The
Captain Justo
Saga

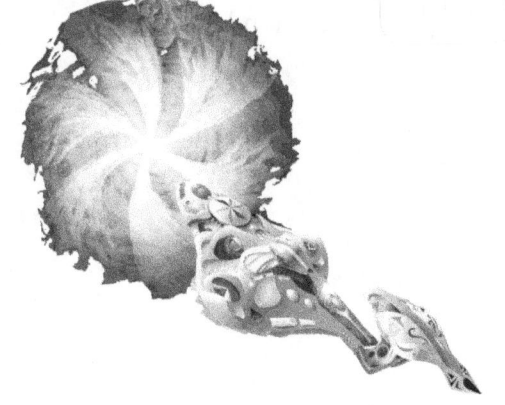

Creating a new universe in the realm of Science Fiction has been a life-changing experience. The eternal rules of the space vortex have redefined my own personal and spiritual journey. I have researched personal empowerment through the social sciences and explored many spiritual traditions. After working for 15 years on developing the Eight Pearls of Is, I discovered that the words of Jesus Christ as recorded in Matthew, Chapter Five, described them best. The Beatitudes influenced their final form.

Stephen Miller

Captain Justo

From the

Planet

Is

Log 1.1

Stephen Miller

Captain Justo from the Planet Is

Fifth Edition August 2010
First Printing

Published by:

V&E Enterprises in partnership with Ivory
Dusk L.C.

Cover Art: Jonathan Hoffman
www.jonpaint.blogspot.com

Edited and typeset: Janet Bernice Jeys
And Valerie J.O. Gardner

ISBN: 978-1-62314-162-2

≈ ACKNOWLEDGMENTS ≈

I would like to thank my wife, Edna. She has been my inspiration and anchor. I must also thank all of my children who have lent me their names and let me take pieces of their personalities and infuse them into my characters. They have influenced every page of this book. It was written for them and about them. I am especially grateful to my son, Daniel, who read every version of my manuscript. His encouragement and love for adventure helped me shape and mold this story to where it is today.

The owners and staff of TriQuest Publishing have been amazing. Their expert advice has made me a better writer. I would also like to thank K. L. Morgan for her moral support and encouraging words over the last 10 years. I would also like to thank Ron Utter who keeps me abreast of all the marketing and publishing possibilities.

Many other people have helped mold and shape this work. I am indebted to Phillip Gleason, Susan Whitenight, and Katherine Hindmarsh. My brothers have been a fountain of ideas and feedback; they're the greatest. Thanks to Gordon Jones, Janet Bernice Jeys and Sheyla Gibbs for their editing contributions. I would also like to thank Georgia Carpenter at Brigham Distributing for taking a chance on an unknown author and bringing me onto her team.

And finally, I would like to offer my sincere appreciation to you; all the people who purchased books from me at fairs, conventions, shopping malls, and at their own doorsteps. Each one of you took a chance on me and I am deeply moved by your generosity and trust. Enjoy this adventure with me; together we can make this world a better place.

Stephen Miller

This is dedicated to my wife and children.

Thank you for letting me turn a bedtime

story into a whole new universe.

❧ Contents ❧

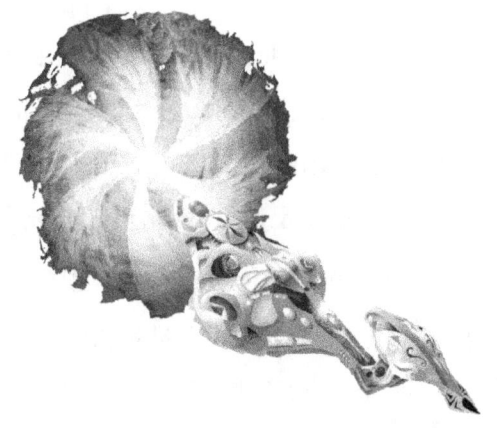

Negotiating With Pirates

The negotiation room was dimly lit with blue photon tubes and flickering static lights. The smell of rotting fish lingered in the damp reprocessed air. The ceiling was low and cluttered with tubes and piping running in every direction. Undecorated metallic walls bore the scars of torpedo blasts, and engine-core meltdowns from an ancient civil war, long since forgotten.

The space station was technically a deep-space military outpost for the Seratian Confederation, but in reality it was nothing more than a grimy salvage operation owned and exploited by a single desperate man. It hung in space like a black six-sided insect with cargo bays and twisted starship scraps poking out of it... unfriendly, uninviting, and dangerous.

The Seratian Confederation guarded the region with unannounced regularity, even though the only living planet was a desolate wasteland covered with the bones and decayed buildings of an ancient civilization long dead. The only inhabitants on the planet were dangerous prisoners who were forced to provide food and supplies for the fleet, which included the floating scrap yard. Officially, the space station was numbered SPS 1366, but the visiting troopers spitefully called it the "Royal Prison Space Station" just as they called the nearby destroyed planet the "Royal Prison Planet."

Inside the room, Admiral Ezra Justo carefully stepped over fish bones and tin cans that were strewn over the grease-stained floor. Spying the only clean spot in the room, he walked towards it. An oak desk with dolphins and flowing water carved into its edges and feet sat in the center of the room. As beautiful as the desk was, its writing surface was strewn with just as many papers and half-eaten meals as the floor. The rest of the room was filled with tables loaded with star charts, computer terminals, and hundreds of blinking lights from plugged-in computer hardware carelessly added on. He regretted that this room would witness the fate of his family's most prized possession.

Admiral Justo was a ninth-generation starship captain, the honorary king of his people, and the rightful Admiral of Kings. His brother, uncles, and cousins were all involved in the same trade: transporting people, information, and supplies to the far reaches of the universe. It paid well, although the Admiral didn't have to work; he had enough crystal in the bank to purchase a fleet of starships together with the crews to man them. Nevertheless, the command of an Isian starship came with the responsibility to work until the blood ceased flowing in the veins. He was glad for that because he liked to work. At 56 Terra years, his hair was now speckled with grey and his build was solid, if a bit round. Yes, the years were starting to show... all the crystal in the universe couldn't stop the onslaught of time.

It was true... time, the enemy of man, was passing quickly for Ezra Justo. Each planet had its own measurement for time, depending on how long it took to revolve around its sun and spin on its own axis, but the only time measurement that he cared about was the 365.242199 days any living planet took to revolve around its sun. Terra time was the living constant in the universe and his body aged at that drum beat.

Ezra reached the clean area of the floor and motioned for his son to come join him. Marion James Justo, the heir to the throne of all Is and the future Admiral of Kings, jumped over the same bones and papers with athletic agility. Marion was 21 years old and had just completed his trials to join his father in the family business. His training culminated in a two-year service assignment to Terra 1154 in the Florin Galaxy, also known as New Euna. During these two unpaid years he dug wells, built schools, and tended to the needs of a gentle people trying to start a new colony. The Admiral admired his son's energy, generosity, and compassion.

"Are you sure they meant to have us meet here?" the young man asked hesitantly. "This space station doesn't have a clean room in it. I wouldn't want to negotiate for even a space scooter in *this* room."

"Just be patient, Marion. I have a feeling this meeting is not exactly public knowledge. If I had to guess - quiet, here they come."

An old, worn out man limped into the room with several younger men following after. The older man had an air of importance, although the rumpled utility space suit he wore didn't give him any dignity. The younger men were covered in grease and soot and their hair was long, unwashed, and scraggly. They were men of hard, dirty work.

They held back by the door and whispered frantically to one another until one stepped reluctantly to the front. "I only sent the transfer of title request but an hour ago," he complained loudly to the leader. "How d' ye expect 'em to give us the clearance to transfer a title so soon? All I have ready is a salvage title, an' why are ye tradin' with an Isian admiral anyway? We're all alone without an official negotiator here... it's madness."

"Keep it shut, boy," the old man growled. "You stand over there and stay out of me way. Don't open yer trap, none of ye. I only have ye here as witnesses. So do yer job and witness, right?"

The three younger men ducked into the shadows and held their peace. The older man limped to the table and, without looking up, cleaned off the desk with the swipe of a large and muscular arm that belied his limp. All the papers, writing tools, and books flew to the floor, adding to the general filthiness of the room.

"It goes like this," he growled. "I'm called Cridoa, son of Cerdic. That dirt bag in the shadows is Ingild the

Lesser - eyes, ears, and yappin' mouth of the Seratian Confederation - and those are his mates. I suppose ye be Admiral Justo, but who's this other pup ye brought with ye? I told ye to come alone. Are ye deaf or just dumb?"

"This is my son, Marion. We stand as one."

"Aye, beggin' yer pardon. A blood son can stand with ye." The old man ducked his head down with respect. "I had a blood son once, and I would that we had him standin' next to me, but I'll not burden ye with that sad story. I found a ship floatin' in me sector, see, and I own the salvage rights for me sector and everything in it. I have complete authority over everything havin' to do with this transaction. Ain't that right, boys?" He looked at the men standing in the corner and they all nodded nervously.

"I done some searchin' and it looks like ye might have an interest in ownin' the pile o' rubbish I found floatin' in me territory. I might have an interest in givin' her to ye for a fair profit. Are ye still interested?"

"I am interested," Admiral Justo said in a dignified way. "We have agreed on a price through our emissaries, and I am ready to make the transfer as you requested."

"Did ye follow me strict instructions, down to the last?" the old man wheezed with a look of craziness in his eyes.

Negotiating With Pirates

"I did as you instructed. I have deposited the digits into your accounts. Do you have the title of the ship with you?"

"O' course I do, do ye think I be off me head?" The old man walked around the table and took out a round ball the size of marble, rolling it in his dirty old hands. "Here's the title, but it's only a salvage title, mind you. Makes the ship worth about as much as a dirty penny, but if'n yer willin' t' trade, then I'm willin' t' take yer money. I think ye be mad though, entering into deep Seratian territory next door, as it were, to the Royal Prison Planet. You must want this piece of floatin' jewelry pretty bad to make this kind a trip. So I'm uppin' me price. I'll take what ye offered, then I'll have another twenty million, in crystal."

"Twenty million in crystal?" young Marion Justo coughed out. "The price has been settled on. What kind of negotiation is this?"

"Keep yer pup shut up, Admiral," the ancient trader barked ferociously as he circled them like a wild animal. "Did ye think ye could waltz into me own back garden and not play by me rules? Did ye think this little transaction was going to come off without a hitch? If so, then ye be the mad ones I'll bet."

Portal One

Admiral Justo motioned for his son to be still. He paused for a moment, then spoke with quiet power and authority.

"I have had many dealings with Seratians in the past and I expect I will have many more in the future. Seratians are men of their word, from the greatest to the weakest. So when you increase the price for the object of our barter by such a significant amount, and in untraceable crystal, there must be a good reason for it. Why do you break your own time-honored vow of fair dealing?"

The old man went pale. His fingers started to shake and a tear leaked from one eye. Then both became as hard as glass. He exploded.

"They stole me son!" he yelled. "Those ungrateful sons of the infernal pit, they recruited him to capture this very ship 40 long years ago, then they lost the ship and me son with it. Is 20 million worth me son? Is a 100 million? You can take yer lousy filthy crystal and sink with it for all I care, but the Seratian Confederation will not have that ship. I won't allow them to get their filthy, connivin' hands on it. I don't know why the Confederation tried to rob it, an' I don't know how they let it slip from their fingers, but for 40 years I've been searching for it, and I finally found it.

Negotiating With Pirates

"I broke into the ship and searched everywhere aboard her. I found no sign of life nor limb, nor corpse of me boy. I found yer cursed golden ship, but not me lad. Now all me hope is gone... he's lost to me. Me tears and me dreams are all dried out like a desert. I only live for revenge, see, and I won't let the Seratian Confederation have the ship. They want it like flies want flesh, but I made up me mind to double cross 'em, to trade it to the only man strong enough to take on the Seratian Confederation and rob her away. That's why I called ye, an' now ye be here. So do you happen to have 20 million in crystal layin' about?"

With those revealing words Ingild the Lesser bolted out of the room and ran down the hall. The other two stood in confusion and shook their heads, their faces pale. Cridoa didn't even try to stop them as they, too, ran out after him.

"And why would I bring another 20 million in crystal to bargain for a ship I already paid 15 million digits to get?"

"Ah, ye want t' know what ye'll be getting for an extra 20 million in untraceable crystal?" He laughed as he looked at Captain Justo intently. "Ye might not get to read about me death, that's what ye get. When the Confederation discovers I sold the Isian to ya I'll be slaughtered before they ever sentence me to life imprisonment. Either way it'll be death. Never again will I sail the wide open reaches of space a free man. But what does that matter? Died, I did, when me son was taken from me. 'Tis only now I begun to live in these last few moments."

"I didn't come to start a war," the Admiral responded. "I came with legitimate papers. I paid with digits through your official Seratian Central Bank. I brought my son to get acquainted with the future duties of the ship's captain."

"Aye, now ye see why I need an extra 20 million in crystal." The old man laughed. "I won't see any of the digits ye paid me through the Seratian Central Bank, and I have to make good on a lot of bribes. The rest of the crystal, let's just say it's going to a worthy cause. I've bribed a judge to give me a lesser sentence if I'm caught, though I'm not sure he'll honor the bribe. But I know this. If I don't hand it over, it'll be the end of me, right?"

"This is unbelievable!" the Admiral exclaimed. "I cannot pay you bribe money. I am Isian. I cannot make deals in the shadows."

"Yet here ye be," The old man smiled. "Ye know our laws be corrupt. Ye know who we are, and why we do what we do. Why do ye act so surprised, dear Admiral? But if ye be surprised, then be quick about it. Me three worthy cohorts weren't in on me little plot. No doubt they're rushin' to turn me in as we speak. They'll be squealin' on me for the reward money, I suspect. Or maybe for the chance to stay alive. That's the biggest reason, I think. I don't blame 'em. So you'd better make a decision. Do ye finish the trade and send me to prison, or do ye not make the trade and see me surely die? I be in yer hands."

A few seconds passed in darkness, then a light came into Admiral Justo's eyes. "I refuse to change the original terms of our agreement. I will not pay you so much as a single crystal for the ship; especially if it's to be used in bribery and illegal activities. However, I am growing rather fond of this desk. I know you are a savvy trader of antiquities. I'm sure you would not part with it for under, say, 20 million."

The old man smiled, watching as the Admiral took out a bag of crystal balls, counted out 20 million in crystal and handed them to him. The old man reached into his dirty pocket, revealed his own crystal, and rolled it on the desk toward Captain Justo.

"That's a good Admiral, ye are. How many men carry around in their pocket a fortune big enough t' make

500 men stinkin' rich? Ye be everythin' ye're supposed to be and more. And just so ya don't think I don't appreciate a man o' yer reputation, I made a log of everythin' I know about the capture of the Isian those long 40 years ago. I stored it on this crystal," he declared as he carefully handed the Admiral the crystal. "I'm hopin' ya might use the ship to find me son, if ye get the chance. That is, if'n ye get out of Seratian territory in one piece, right?"

"How much time do we have?" Admiral Ezra Justo asked smartly as he put the title to the space ship safely in his coat pocket.

"I'd say about three days if yer lucky, two days if yer unlucky, and about four hours if everythin' turns out like I expect it to."

"Then we don't have a moment to lose."

"Good luck then." The old man chuckled. "I'm sorry ye have to run. An' don't forget yer desk. 'Tis a shame though, I liked that desk."

"Twenty million in crystal!" Marion exclaimed once they were securely inside their own transporter. "Why would you have 20 million in crystal ready to give to a Seratian Pirate? I thought this was a normal business negotiation!"

Negotiating With Pirates

"It's family business," the admiral said solemnly as they sailed at half port speed toward the salvage bay where the spaceship was stored. "The Isian isn't an ordinary space ship, son. It's our family's most valuable possession. Inside that ship are centuries of irreplaceable craftsmanship, art, and history. That would be worth risking our lives for alone, but there's more. Our family's honor is on the line. I would have given the old trader a hundred million in crystal, if he had asked for it."

As they drew close to the salvage bay they were joined by two other small transport ships. One was a barge from the Salvage Space Station, the other a schooner from the Argo, Admiral Justo's starship. The salvage barge verified the impound release order and authenticated the salvage title. A few minutes passed uneasily, but then the massive blast doors began to swing open. As they did, the lights from the salvage barge shone on the dark, shrouded vessel. When the doors were fully opened, the space barge entered the bay and unlocked the seal holding the Isian securely to the space station. The ship drifted freely, without power, and needed help from the salvage barge to keep it from hitting the sides of the bay.

The salvage barge steadied the dead ship, slowly pulling it out of its hiding place. Several crew members exited the barge in space suits and jet packs, floating to remove the covering that veiled the condition of the ship.

Marion's heart raced. This was the first time they had had a chance to look at the impounded starship. The hidden shape of the ship began to take form as sheets of protective padding were stripped away from the hull. Piece by piece the cover was removed, revealing a spectacular, perfect starship. It was breathtaking. Instead of being made from industrial-grade gold like the Argo, the Isian was crafted with the highest grade of fine ceremonial gold... crafted after the ancient Alpha Class design, with swept-back wings and an arcing tail rising high above the body of the ship.

"Did you know the Isian was Alpha Class?" Marion asked his equally excited father.

"I did," The Admiral confirmed, "and a lot more. Your grandfather inherited the Isian 40 years ago after the tragic, early death of your great-grandfather. He tried to complete his father's last scheduled mission, but lost the ship to Seratian Pirates on his very first voyage. It was such a shock he refused to captain another ship. I asked him about it once when I was 10 and received a spanking like I'd never experienced before. Later, he admitted he was mortified by his behavior and said I could ask any question I wanted, but I was too hurt to ask again."

"This situation is already more complicated than I ever imagined." He closed his eyes for a second, sighed then put his hand on Marion's shoulder. "I shouldn't have brought you along; your mother would be frantic if she knew how much danger we are in."

"I can handle this," his son insisted, "I know a lot more about piloting a starship than you give me credit for. I can do this."

"I believe you can." Admiral Justo confirmed. "That's why I agreed to let you come. I needed someone I could trust with my life."

Just then an encoded transmission report came from the bridge of the starship Argo. "Here is the status report," Admiral Aaron Justo announced. "There is a Seratian star destroyer three days away, bound for the space station. They have long-range fighters that could be here in 24 hours if they want to send them. They also have fighter probes that could make the voyage sooner than that. I don't know how badly the Seratian Confederation wants the ship but from your experience in the negotiation room earlier today, I'd say they want it pretty badly."

"Any suggestions," the Admiral asked.

"We can tie the Isian to the Argo and sail her far enough away to give us time to get her ready to pass through the Chanson Vortex. Any vortex will suit our purposes, but I think the Chanson Vortex is flowing at the strongest frequency right now."

"Begin the procedure," the Admiral agreed, "Keep me informed of any changes."

"I do trust you son," the Admiral said proudly. "While the rest of the crew attaches the tow bar to the ship, I need you inside, initiating the start-up sequence. Once the command center computers are booted up, we can see what kind of damage we have. There is a chance the vortex drives are still operational. If they are, I need you to get them ready. So suit up, son, I need you in there now."

"Thanks Admiral," Marion said happily. "I won't let you down.

"You have to know one more thing," his father added. "Be careful, leave when I say leave, and I love you."

"That's three things," Marion smiled and gave his Dad a strong embrace. "I'll be careful."

Marion ran to the transporter bay and slipped on his silver protective coat. He was about to don his helmet when an explosion rattled the Argo's small shuttle craft. He looked out the window in time to see a portion of the space station erupt in flames, spewing metal and glass into the airless night. The salvage workers also saw the explosion. Without removing the remainder of the protective coverings from the Isian, they quickly jetted to the salvage barge, entered the stout craft, unhooked it from the Isian, and darted away toward the wounded space station.

"We're on our own," Admiral Justo called over his communicator to the Argo. "Major Alden, get the schooner in position; we're going to have to tug the Isian away from the space station ourselves. Send a crew out to remove the rest of the covering. We don't have much time."

"We can still do this," the Admiral said to himself, opening a communication link to his son. "As soon as we have the ship secured by the schooner you get in there and check out the vortex drive. I'm heading back to the *Argo* to get the tow bars ready. Can you do this?"

"I can!" Marion said confidently, "just get everything else ready and I'll have the computers up."

The Admiral looked out the window only to see another portion of the space station rocked by a massive explosion. "They'll be after us next," the Admiral lamented. "I hope that 20 million in crystal was enough. I should have given Cridoa more to bribe his own staff. Go now, Marion; I'll see you back at the Argo. Please be careful. That's an order."

Marion secured his round helmet and floated his way to the back of the ship. He closed the air lock and unlatched a jet pack from the side of the bay. Donning the pack, he took a mighty lunge from the bay door. He aimed all his weight for the X on the back of the shuttle, which opened like the iris of an eye when he came close to it. He floated into open space and activated the jet pack which vibrated into full life.

"I'm ship-bound, Admiral," the young Justo announced. "Permission to board the Isian?"

"Permission granted," his father responded through his helmet communicator. "Your voice patterns are now programmed to activate all systems on the Isian. You are captain. Good luck."

Portal Two

Seratian Attack

Marion steered his jet pack toward the helpless Isian and flew full speed to the docking port. He looked over his shoulder long enough to see his father's transporter dart away into the star-strewn emptiness of deep space. When he arrived at the docking port, he searched around until he found the hand-sized opening containing a manual lever to open a way into the ship. He put his hand into the opening and tugged on the lever. A smooth vibration tickled his fingers as he felt the mechanics inside the ship come to life.

Seconds later a door opened into the air lock. Marion pushed himself into the opening and the door quickly closed behind him. Still weightless, he took off his jet pack, attached it to a waiting hanger, then floated on up to the control panel. He entered several commands and the airlock hissed with warm vapor. After a quick test, he knew it was safe to take off his helmet and breathe. An explosion from outside rocked the ship. He sighed with relief, realizing that at least he'd made it inside safely.

Still floating, he grabbed the handles next to the control panel and made his request to enter. "I am Marion James Justo, son of Ezra James Justo, son of Marion Thomas Justo, requesting permission to enter the ship. Do you recognize?" A light flashed green, indicating the door was ready to open. Not knowing what the interior temperature of the ship would be, he quickly put his helmet back on and pushed the button. The door opened smoothly, revealing the black interior of the ship.

"Activate emergency power," the young captain commanded. The ship responded by lighting up the entry way with brilliant red lights. "Activate emergency gravitational systems." At his command a band of lights glowed on his own golden space boots. "Stabilize," he commanded, and the boots floated firmly to the floor. When they made contact, a line of floor lights clicked on down the hall and out of sight.

"Ship's navigation and layout computer, respond." A musical tone filled the room and Marion smiled. "Lead the way to the command center."

He ran forward along the port of the ship until he saw a spiral staircase going four levels topside. But before running up the stairs he looked down at his boots and gave another quick command. "Motion boost," he yelled; then instead of stepping a stair at a time, he easily hurtled up three steps with each leap. When he cleared the last stair he ran to the closed door, which opened at his command. "Captain's chair activate," he said as he entered the large command center. A chair in the middle of the room came to life, spinning, beckoning him to sit and take control. Another vibration jolted the ship causing the frame to groan.

"Initiate startup sequence."

The chair moved into its forward position and a large, organ-like control panel came up from the floor and surrounded him. "DNA verification activate," he said as he took off his glove and placed his hand on the frigid panel; it lit up in response to his touch. He removed his hand from the lights and positioned them on a keyboard.

"Ionic engines, engage." A roar came from inside the ship as the red emergency lights instantly turned brilliant white. Motors, fans, and the sound of rushing water all worked together as if the ship were being aroused from a deep slumber. And finally the air in the command center started to circulate, bringing with it the feeling of warmth.

Marion watched a temperature gauge on the initiation sequence panel as it went from 60 below freezing to an acceptable 20 below. He took off his helmet, gasping at the cold air rushing into his lungs. *Cold, but not too cold*, he thought, catching his breath.

"Command shield screens open."

The shields covering the windows of the command center retracted in time to reveal an entire section ripped from the space station. What was happening at the Salvage Space Station was nothing less than war. His fingers raced on the keys as fast as his heart pounded in his chest... neither could perform a beat faster.

"Communication links up," he said urgently.

The sound of his father's voice came screeching over the speakers, "Are you up, are you up?"

"I'm operational, Admiral," Marion shouted. "The initiation sequence is 15 percent complete, and so far all systems seem to be perfect. I don't see anything wrong. How soon before the schooner can tow me out of here?"

Seratian Attack

"There's no time for that, son," his father said frantically. "Cridoa just sent me a posting telling me he has bought us all the time he can. He is falling back with everyone loyal to him and abandoning the Salvage Space Station. They are heading to Fredonia, a space port on the Royal Prison Planet to try to find some protection there. We are on our own. I have instructed the men in your hanger to fall back to the schooner and I'm ordering you to come with them."

"We are Isian, Dad," Marion called back. "We can't let Seratian pirates take whatever they want. For some reason this ship means a lot to them. Let's not just give it up."

"It's not worth your life. I can replace a starship; I can't replace you."

"Wait a minute Dad, there might be another way. I just made it through 25 percent of the initializing sequence. I don't have navigation thrusters, but I have plenty of raw power. If the schooner pointed me in the right direction, I'm sure I can fly her out of here. It doesn't matter where I sail, as long as it's away from the spaceport. Just steer me clear of the station, then you can catch up with me. It could work. This is worth more than an office desk. Let's do it."

Portal Two

Reluctantly, Admiral Justo agreed. The schooner pulled next to the Isian, gently nudging it away from the spaceport. Marion looked over toward the space station as it continued to flash and tremble and watched ships darting away from it in every direction - all except for one - moving purposefully toward him.

"You're clear, son," his father announced. "The schooner will track you. Make this sharp, you have a salvage barge closing in on you."

"Prepare aft thrusters," Marion commanded. The engines of the Isian let out a trembling groan, as if 40 years of inactivity bottled up inside waited to be released. "Activate on my mark: three, two, one, activate!"

The thrusters screamed into life, sending a stream of blue ions into the void. The power of the blast caused the salvage barge to spin out of control and ram harmlessly into the salvage bay. The schooner darted forward at the same time, leaving behind its own ion wake, then trailed the Isian as closely as it dared.

Inside the Isian, Captain Justo held on to his seat with all of his strength. Without any acceleration protection, his body was forced to endure the full brunt of the gravitational forces caused by the ship's thrusters. Nimble and powerful, the engines easily distanced him from the visual image of the space station. Three minutes passed, and the acceleration from the powerful engines caused the ship to pitch and roll until the frame of the starship groaned under the stress. Without directional thrusters the ship was in danger of being ripped apart by the engines' uncontrolled maneuvers. He had to act fast.

"Thru-u-usters diseng-gage," he gasped with his last full breath, but he could only manage a dry, airless whisper. The ship's computer was unable to perceive his vocal command. With almost no ability to breathe, he could feel the strength ebbing from his body. His vision narrowed and his head throbbed, but with all his remaining energy he placed his hands on the keyboard, sending the ship one last command before passing out.

The thrusters immediately shut down, leaving the ship drifting aimlessly at half the speed of light. Aboard the schooner, the crew was able to keep the out-of-control Isian in her scope. While more than once the Isian burst out of tracking range, it was only due to the skills of the schooner's navigator that they were able to re-establish contact.

After several hours, a rescue team was able board the ship, bringing her under control. They found Marion passed out in the captain's chair. They took him directly to the captain's quarters located off the Command Center and let him rest. His eardrums were nearly ruptured and he suffered from severe vertigo, but the med-tech insisted he would recover quickly.

While Marion's health was being stabilized the rescue party sent their location to the crew of the Argo. A short hour later the three ships met, rejoicing in their good fortune.

When Marion woke up four hours later, he looked up into the smiling faces of his father and uncle. Looking about, he saw that the room was ornately decorated with woodwork of intertwining leaves and flowers. He blinked and squinted to shield his eyes from the light.

"Where am I?"

"You're in the captain's quarters of the Isian," His father explained. "I didn't think it would be right to relieve you of your command while you were unconscious, so I ordered the ship's surgeon to put you and all your gear in the captain's quarters and let you rest up. How do you like it, son?"

"The captain's quarters? Why would you put my gear in the captain's quarters? I thought you were going to give the command to Uncle Aaron, I mean, Admiral Aaron Justo?"

"After what I saw you do today, you deserve to be in the captain's quarters. Besides, after the initiation sequence was complete, the main computer wouldn't recognize any other captain. It's an old computer program; I guess it only recognizes one captain at a time."

"I don't mind," Admiral Aaron Justo smiled. "I have a fleet of starships back home. I just came along in case there was any trouble. If I had known how well you think on your feet I might not have come. You just get better, Captain Justo," he said with deliberate emphasis.

* * * * * * * * * *

Back on the burning salvage station, Inglid the Lesser opened up a communication link with Admiral Albrecht of the Seratian Confederation.

"I did what ye commanded and me whole world is burnin' up."

"Did you capture the Isian?" the Admiral demanded over the transmitter. "Just tell me you maintained control of the Isian."

"No sir, we didn't. The salvage station's in flames; we're at war. Cridoa, the mangy beast, had explosives planted all over the station and he's blown the world up. I'm lucky to be wearing me space suit or I'd have me insides splattered all over the walls. Now, the question is, are ye goin' to honor our deal and give me the 50 thousand in crystal?"

"You'll get your crystal, Inglid," Admiral Albrecht assured him. "We're Seratian. We always trade square. Find out which direction they took the Isian, and I'll give you 500,000 in crystal, and the title to the whole salvage operation. Our battle group will arrive in two days time. Make sharp, Captain Inglid."

"Aye, Admiral," Inglid grunted and let out a cry of glee. "Do you hear that, you bags of spoiled meat? I'm the boss. Save the livin' quarters, and put a team on saving the segment with the deep space antenna. The station's been damaged a-plenty, but it can all be fixed. We have some ion trails to follow. Look sharp or I'll gut your oxygen lines wide open. We have major brass on the way and we don't want ta disappoint 'em."

* * * * * * * * *

Two days passed quickly aboard the Isian. As soon as his strength returned, Marion worked alongside the other men. Fresh supplies were transferred from the Argo, enough to outfit a crew of 12 for a year's travel time-bound; and the ion fuel rods were replaced to ensure the safety of the ship. The Argo kept close watch on the damaged Salvage Space Station, although the captain took care not to reveal their location.

The time aboard the stationary Isian wasn't wasted. While waiting for more supplies Marion spent long hours walking the halls and rooms with his father. They shared the discovery together, learning about the artwork, the handcrafted woodwork, and the true purpose of the ship.

"This ship has been in the family for 10 generations," Admiral Justo explained as they admired the ship. "She has been used as a portable cathedral, traveling to the far reaches of the universe, offering a place for Isian's to perform knighting, coronation, and marriage ceremonies. A finely seasoned musical instrument couldn't be more precious."

As they went from floor to floor, Marion learned that the Isian was first of the standard Alpha Class Starships. It had four decks on the main level and one deck high above the rest of the ship aloft. In the center of the ship a giant cargo hold would normally extend all the way to the top of the ship. But in the Isian, the cargo hold was divided into smaller rooms connecting into one large ceremonial room with seating for hundreds of people. The ceiling extended like a cathedral and the windows on top, when the blast shields were open, sprinkled light on the participants like stardust.

The center of the ship was surrounded by a hall on both sides with utility rooms and crew quarters housed inside the graceful wings of the ship. At the trailing edge of the wings, on both sides, were rows of very special crystal bowls. These bowls were placed one inside another so close they almost touched. The bowls rotated along a center axis when activated and, if touched by a moist leather pad, they rang out a musical pitch so perfect and powerful it caused the whole ship to vibrate. When harmonic cords were played in specific sequences the very matter around the ship danced with delight.

As with all Isian spacecraft, the harmonics of the crystal bowls were the reason Isians could travel outside of time and space and visit the far reaches of the universe. All Isians were taught from an early age that each star, planet, and moon has a musical tone and that by combining those specific tones it was possible to harmonically or musically describe the specific location of any object in space.

It was during an in-flight rehearsal of the Interplanetary Symphony by Gustoff Brenhardt, based on the tonal quality linking two closely positioned star systems, that the whole ship was transported from one star system to another. Unfortunately, only two members survived the voyage unharmed: the ship's chaplain and a violinist named Albert James Justo. The others were permanently disabled or killed. The Interplanetary Symphony became the object of intense scientific study. Experiments were conducted and it was discovered that wormholes were more than random strings in space-time - they were living Rivers of Eternity. These strings were attracted to music and could be summoned and navigated.

Albert James Justo, the violinist, purchased an old cargo ship and started doing experiments with it. He dared to enter and exit the wormhole that connected the two star systems. He referred to the worm holes as Rivers of Eternity, and later as space vortices. He exhausted his entire family fortune with a final experiment on how to make the vortices safe for others to navigate.

He reasoned that if the ship were protected by a seamless coat of gold, the occupants would have a better chance of surviving the effects of the vortex. Gold was a pure element that the space vortex favored over other metals because gold acted as a shield. The space vortex was alive like a person—moving, changing, and choosing whom it wanted to let enter its river of energy. Once inside, all time stood still and distance lost all meaning. Everything that decayed was restored again and all machines that needed to use energy stopped functioning, including the human body.

What Albert Justo discovered inside the space vortex was that the soul or spirit of a traveler took a more physical form and could keep the body functioning during the voyage. A spirit could become dim and powerless if the laws of the universe were not followed during regular day-to-day living. Thus, if a person didn't follow these laws, he could not survive a trip through the vortex. These laws corresponded to the teachings of a remarkable teacher known as The Great Is. Those who diligently followed the laws of Is could travel through the vortex, and those who didn't... could not.

In one daring trip Albert sailed 100 million light years from his own star, marked his position, and returned again with his crew unharmed. He christened his cargo ship the Isian, Alpha Class. It was the first ship to sail in the Rivers of Eternity and come out with a living crew. It was also the first ship to be covered completely in pure gold to withstand the searing heat of the pure energy and intelligence. At the helm, Captain Albert Justo was the first to discover and refine the rules of Eternal Space Travel and master its intricacies. And for that discovery he was given the title Albert the Just, Admiral of the Space Vortex. Even though it was ceremonial, the family took its royal charter seriously.

It took a new way of life to travel the Rivers of Eternity. A good personal character was required, not just technical ability. Those who mastered these traits became the rulers of a new society of space travelers. Vortex space travel redefined their families, their culture, and their very existence. This personal commitment is what made them so different from the Seratian pirates aboard the Salvage Space Station and the men inside the slow time-bound destroyer that had just docked at the still-smoldering floating station. The men and women who learned to navigate the Rivers of Eternity came to be known as Isians, or the people of Is.

When they finished their tour, Marion looked out at the immensity of space and felt a little more connected to it. "Does Grandpa Justo still have the title Admiral of Kings?" he asked.

"No, He refused the honor," Admiral Justo said sadly. "When I came of age, I took the title for the family. I'm hoping to pass it on to you someday."

"Well," Marion smiled, "let's just hope that won't happen for a good long time."

Portal Two

As they walked into the command center of the ship Ezra Justo left his role as father behind and became Admiral Justo again. "How far are we from an entry point to the Chanson Vortex?" he asked Lieutenant Julian Franco, his navigator.

"We are still about three terra days out from a full frequency entrance sir, although I am getting intermittent signals from it right now."

"That's good to hear. Keep your eyes bright, Lieutenant. I don't know how much more time we have before we'll have to start running."

"The Seratian Confederation destroyer just arrived at the Salvage Space Port," he reported. "I'm sure every ionic particle we emit is being searched for right now."

Admiral Justo nodded and walked back to his own intricate command chair and hailed the Argo on a secure line. "Hailing Admiral Aaron Justo, are you there?"

"Yes, Admiral," His brother responded. "I hear you loud and clear."

"Lieutenant Franco informs me we are nearing the entrance to the Chanson Vortex. Are you getting readings as well?"

"Weak ones," he replied. "Not enough to travel into. What's the status of your ship?"

Seratian Attack

"All systems have been tested except for the starboard vortex drive. I just finished with the tests on the port drive and everything looks fine. We should be operational in a few hours." "That's good," the Admiral Aaron Justo said with relief. "I have studied the information provided by Cridoa on the space station and I have downloaded it to you on a secure line. According to this report, Cridoa was once a programmer for the Seratian Royal House, the ruling government before the rise of the Seratian Confederation. His teenage son, Cenric, worked with him and was a brilliant programmer, exceeding even his father's abilities. King Elfwald and his queen, Mathilda, were studying with Lorenzo Justo, your grandfather, to be an Isian star captain, and this made many members of the ruling family uncomfortable, especially his nephew, Prince Alhred. They feared if he became an Isian he would use his power and influence to force everyone to become Isian and they would lose their status in the kingdom.

Admiral Justo turned to Marion and explained further. "This is the time when Admiral Lorenzo Justo, my grandfather was accidently killed in an industrial accident aboard the Royal Space Port. He was loading a shipment of medicine in its small cargo bay when the boxes fell and crushed him. Your grandfather was only 21 when that happened and he decided to finish the training of King Elfwald."

"According to this," Aaron Justo continued, "Prince Alhred apparently enlisted the aid of the young programmer Cenric to capture the Isian when it was docked at the Royal Space Port and kidnapped the king's son, Prince Sevan. In the ransom negotiations it was calculated that the king would give up his intentions to be an Isian and all would be well. According to Seratian Law all of this intrigue is completely within the right of an upcoming heir to the throne.

"Things went as planned at first. The security detail at the Royal Space Port and those on the Isian were tricked by Prince Alhred and his men while your grandfather was being honored at a feast in the Royal Space Station. First of all, the ship was fired on and successfully defended. Later, after the feast, and after the Isian's crew thought all was well, the Isian set sail to meet with King Elfwald for his first training mission. On the way she was overcome by the pirates who sailed into deep space with Cenric the programmer, a small crew, and Prince Sevan. King Elfwald was furious and ordered every ship in his garrison to search and bring the ship back safely."

"I know what happened next," Marion broke in. "With all the royal security searching for the Isian, Prince Alhred rallied his men and captured the king with all his sympathizers, accused them of sedition for trying to become Isian, and sent them to the Royal Prison Planet."

"That's right son," his father confirmed. "And the Isian was never seen again. A half-mad crew was found floating in an escape pod not far from here; but Cenric, the young programmer, and Sevan, the king's son, were not among them. Prince Alhred proclaimed himself protector until the lost prince was recovered. If this information got out it could rally support for the royal family on the Royal Prison Planet. We have to get all of this back home to analyze it in more detail and confirm it with the Isian's ship logs. No wonder the Seratian Confederation is willing to do so much to recover the Isian. We need to get this ship fully operational. I need to get back to the Argo, can you get the starboard vortex drive tuned?"

"I'll head down to the crystal room right now," the young captain said earnestly. "I'll have to turn off my communicator for an hour while I calibrate the crystals, but I'll check in as soon as I'm done."

"I can't think of anyone I trust more than you, son," he said proudly. "Contact me as soon as you are done."

"As soon as I'm done," Marion assured him, running out the door.

Hiding behind a shroud of darkness, deadly Seratian star fighters moved in ever closer.

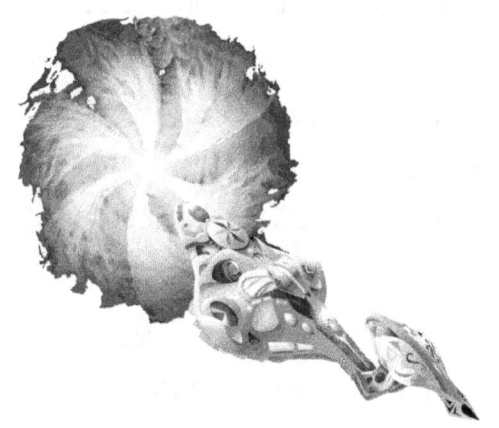

Into the River of Fire

Captain Justo entered the long room of circular crystal bowls. The entry door was located where the wing connected to the main fuselage of the ship. The room extended the full length of the wing, rounding outward as the wing rounded and becoming narrower as it neared the wing's tip. The first bowl was a massive 20 feet in diameter and three inches thick. The next bowl fit neatly inside and was just slightly smaller, and so on, each bowl becoming smaller and smaller until at the end they were as small and thin as a thimble.

Marion took out his calibration tools and ordered the organ-like command chair to activate, but nothing happened. He spoke the command again, but it still didn't respond to his voice. Getting a little frustrated he reached down and manually tried to activate the keyboard, but it wouldn't operate. He opened a service panel and peered inside. Nothing seemed damaged, but when he tested a few connections he found the whole assembly was completely without power.

Frantic now, he pulled up a schematic for the ship on his handheld device and found the location of the main box that controlled the power for the starboard vortex drive. Searching the wall he found the blast door of the service room and pried the heavy door open. He commanded the interior light to illuminate, but it wouldn't. He peered into the darkness, but without light he couldn't see anything. He tried the manual switch but it was also dead.

All the power in the room is connected to the same source, he reasoned.

He pulled a portable light from a pack he brought with him and shone it into the dark utility room. The powerful light shone on floor and on the small boxy custodial robots connected to the side of the wall. It illuminated closet doors and shallow sinks, all perfectly normal, but in the corner of the room it shone on a golden figure slouching on the ground next to an open control panel. Strands of electrical wiring were hanging all over the golden figure.

"Stay away," it blurted out in a drunken voice.

Suddenly, the sound of an emergency siren vibrated through the whole ship and the robotic intruder turned its head and lurched forward.

Marion was taken by surprise and fell backward on his bag of instruments. The robot leaped forward and was about to land on top of him when he was pulled back by electrical cords connected to his chest. At the same time the heavy blast door closed tight and the sound of the siren became muffled, as if it were a distant memory.

"Must save the ship!" the robot said frantically. "Intruders, pirates, Seratians, must... save... the ship..."

As he talked, his power cells drained to the end of their energy reserves and the robot fell lifeless to the ground.

"It's a navigator," Captain Justo said in astonishment. "I didn't think any of them were still operational."

The navigator, a robot covered in solid gold, looked like a six-foot tall man with a humanoid face and a helmet for hair. The outer covering looked like a space suit out of a museum, with flexible joints and red-gold boots. His hands and face were of a different alloy of gold and they looked silvery-white. Sparks were coming from the wires he had been patched into and, with a simple test, Justo deducted they were the power supply to the whole vortex drive.

Marion tried to open the blast door, but it was jammed shut. Without power he was trapped, so he carefully rewired the control box and the whole room came alive. He didn't know what made him more excited, finding another piece to the ship's puzzle or getting the vortex drive activated. He searched through his supplies and quickly found a power cord, which he attached to the robot. As the robot's batteries were charging he opened the service room blast door and listened for the emergency sirens. They were no longer blaring; they must have been caused by the robot.

Now he focused all of his attention on calibrating the crystal bowls of the vortex drive. Forty-five minutes passed; Captain Justo kept his hand-held communicator off so they would not interfere with his calibrations. When he finished a successful test he connected the system to the main computer and turned on his hand-held.

"Admiral, the vortex drive is operational, do you copy?"

Into the River of Fire

"Where have you been?" a frantic voice answered him.

"I'm in the starboard vortex drive room. I had to turn off my hand-held communicator. Don't you remember?"

"I sent Major Alden down to the starboard vortex drive room to find you; you weren't there. We've been searching for you everywhere. I finally had to order the complete evacuation of the ship and try to fight our way out of this."

"I didn't have any power," Marion quickly explained. "I was trapped in a utility closet for about 20 terra-minutes. I heard the emergency siren but I thought it was part of the drive malfunction. What's happening?"

"We're under attack, Marion. We have already destroyed three deep space missiles and we're tracking 10 more. A fully-armed Seratian destroyer has already launched her fighters to intercept us. They are not offering terms of surrender, they're after blood. There's no time to lose. We don't have time to save the Isian. Now that you are found we're going to let the high-energy torpedoes destroy her and make a run for the Chanson Vortex. We are already preparing to enter."

"But we have clear title. Even by their pirate laws we own the ship. They can do what they want to that old man, but he traded it to us fair and square."

"You're not seeing the seriousness of the situation," cried Admiral Justo. "This is an act of war. All the normal rules of trade are null and void. The Isian is going to be the first casualty of this aggressive action and they won't stop... launch the torpedo now... put the shields up. Brace yourselves!"

A huge explosion came over the head set and the Isian rocked violently from the blast. "That was a near hit. Good shot, Aaron! Marion, get off that ship; use an escape pod, that's an order!"

Suddenly, the once dormant robot stumbled out of the utility room. "We're under attack," it said, and ran to the vortex drive command center.

"Engaging the vortex drive," it said in a crackling voice, followed by a thousand booming sounds echoing from inside the belly of the robot.

"What are you doing?" Marion stammered. "I have to get out of here. There's no time to test the vortex drive. We have to get in an escape pod."

"No time for that, sir," the navigator robot responded, still emitting intricate rhythms and musical tones. "An approaching fighter just launched a high-energy torpedo at us; it should make contact in 20 terra-seconds. You wouldn't make it to the escape pods before we were blown out of the sky. Brace yourself. Engaging emergency vortex drive start-up."

"Get to an escape pod," Admiral Justo ordered over the intercom. "You've been targeted by a fighter. Get out of there!"

Marion could hear the panic in his father's voice. He ran out of the room and left the robot at the vortex command center. He opened his hand-held and commanded it to show him the security situation of the ship. He verified the fighter had launched three high energy torpedoes at him, with an expected detonation in 10 terra-seconds.

"I love you Dad," he yelled into his communicator, "It's too late... I can't leave."

"Get back into the utility closet and engage the blast door. We still have a chance to save you. I'll surrender and send in a rescue team."

Marion ran back to the vortex drive room. "The torpedo's going to hit us in five seconds. Get in the storage room."

The navigator replied calmly, "We have plenty of time. Engaging vortex drive, now." The room came alive with a full harmonic symphony. Light danced off the crystal bowls like rippling water as the chords vibrated through the hull of the ship and created a blue hue that surrounded the whole craft. The energy completely blocked all sense of reality and a peaceful feeling enveloped the captain as its searing heat filled his heart.

"They've been hit," a trembling voice said over the intercom.

"We've been hit," the young captain repeated as he felt the ship rock from the blast. The first high-energy torpedo grazed the skin of the Isian and exploded on impact making a small breach in the ship's protective golden hull and causing emergency lights to flash.

Marion looked at his hand-held in horror, another two torpedoes were seconds behind. Marion prepared himself for another impact.

Suddenly, the room filled with a roiling circle of fire, distorting his sense of reality. The music from the bowls exploded in a massive symphony, just like the missiles that would surely bend and warp the hull of the ship until there was nothing left.

The walls blared and groaned with the ferocity of trumpets. Sparks radiated and danced in the air and waves of red and green radiation penetrated every molecule of

Marion's body. His heart stopped pumping blood; his lungs stopped breathing in oxygen. He looked at his hands and saw them start to turn blue as tiny stars began to appear in his peripheral vision.

With his last spark of life, he looked over at the golden navigator and expected to see him exploding into tiny pieces, but instead the robot was merely thrown to the floor. Another few breathless moments passed; then Marion turned to see the interior of the long vortex drive completely filled with swirling rings of fire; green and red radiation waves like rainbows danced across the room.

So this is what it's like to die.

Pain tore through his chest as if each molecule was gasping for life. His head felt like it would burst. Panic gripped him as he felt his life force leaking out of him. Several more moments passed and though the ship was still intact, his pain intensified. Muscles cramped and contracted, sending Marion crouching to the floor in pain. He writhed in agony, his torture suspended in space… frozen, exquisite, eternal. Another minute or day or year went by and he began to beg for death. He yearned for the peace he believed should come. Why was he still in ultimate pain and why was the ship still intact? While he suffered in intense agony, the rest of his surroundings danced with twirling fire, light, and music.

"You're right, son," said a voice from the spiraling fire. "You're not dead. If you were dead one of us would come and greet you, keep you safe, protect you from the suffering you're experiencing. You're traveling unprotected in a space vortex, like I did many centuries ago. Few can survive a voyage, but you can."

"You can do it," another pillar of fire encouraged him.

"Yes, you can," said another, until he was surrounded with hundreds of spinning whirling vortices, all calling out words of encouragement and life.

"I can't bear the pain," Marion groaned, managing to work his lungs with all the effort he could muster.

"Yes you can," the first, most brilliant pillar of fire assured him. "You are my blood, my heir, the captain of the ship I built. You must repair the breach in the hull, seek out those that are lost and bring them back to their proper universe. The fate of our family lies in the balance. Farewell." The swirling flame burned even more brilliantly, then spun right through the hull of the ship.

"Where will I find them?" Marion whispered softly. "How will I know who they are?"

Into the River of Fire

"You'll know," a woman's voice comforted him softly from a spinning ball of flames. "You'll know." She, too, became a brilliant vortex of fire and was about to leave the room when somehow Marion was able to peer into the fiery flame and see a beautiful woman wrapped in linen standing on a plate of pure gold. She looked back at him and smiled. "You are a special one, aren't you?"

In a flash, a hundred men and women came into his view, all surrounded in brilliant white, more glorious than the light of the sun at noon day. Their countenance was hotter than a furnace and more pure than the whitest snow. Their hands and feet were bare and they all stood on plates of pure gold.

"Farewell," they called softly. Encircling him with light and fire they darted out in all directions, taking the shimmering green and red rainbows with them. The room went dark and lifeless, but the music of the crystal bowls still rang.

Am I in heaven? he thought, awestruck. Am I really dead after all?

A peaceful feeling came over him, and he realized he was both safe *and* alive. The emergency lights inside the long room began to flicker. He felt the effects of time and decay coming back into his body. Life filled his being, blood rushed through his veins, and oxygen filled his lungs. He was, indeed, mortal again.

Marion couldn't judge how long the Isian had traveled inside the stream of the space vortex. Traveling outside of space-time was uncertain business. A voyage of only a few light years could seem to take hours, while a voyage of millions of light years could seem to take only seconds. The intensity of the pain he experienced had made the trip seem like years.

The biggest fear of any space vortex traveler was to have a breach in the protective golden covering of the ship. A breach, no matter how small, would expose the passengers to the full effects of the stream of pure intelligence, and was certain death for all but the most powerful. It was too dangerous to experiment with even in theory. No human within the last 10 generations had traveled the Rivers of Eternity unprotected. He felt fortunate to be alive. He crawled over to the command station, collapsed in its soft padded leather seat, and fell instantly asleep.

* * * * * * * * *

"He's been hit," Admiral Ezra Justo's voice was strained. "He's been entirely destroyed." All the crew aboard the starship Argo bowed their heads in reverence and shock except for Lieutenant Franco, a junior officer who kept staring at the monitor looking for signs of life in the debris. He had witnessed the torpedo burst into the side of the Isian, but knew something was wrong, at least something didn't make any sense. If the Isian had been destroyed where was the wreckage? All he could identify were several panels of golden ship hull twisted into snarled shrapnel and pieces of the destroyed missile; he couldn't see anything else on the monitor. He started to run another test when he tracked two high-energy torpedoes passing right through the site where the wreckage of the Isian should have been.

"L-look, look at this, Admiral," Lieutenant Franco stuttered. "Two high-energy torpedoes just passed through the wreckage site of the Isian and are coming this way."

"Through the wreckage site of the Isian?" Admiral Aaron Justo repeated in disbelief. "High-energy torpedoes are so sensitive they'll explode in a stellar dust cloud. How could they pass through the mass of a destroyed starship without hitting something?"

"My instruments aren't showing any debris in the last known location of the Isian," Lieutenant Franco responded. "It's like they've vanished, or maybe they were picked up by a space vortex?"

Portal Three

"Impossible," Admiral Ezra Justo thundered.

Finally, getting control of his emotions, he said, "We are still too far away from the Chanson Vortex to get picked up."

"It wasn't the Chanson Vortex that picked them up. There were strong readings from another vortex, one I've never seen before. It's gone now, though. Somehow the Isian was taken up by an uncharted vortex... maybe he survived."

"Is that possible?" Ezra cried. "Let me look at the data."

He pulled the information up on his own computer console and sure enough, residual vortex readings were off the charts.

"The two torpedoes have locked on our harmonics, Admiral," Lieutenant Franco informed. "Permission to launch a counter-missile attack?"

"Permission granted," Admiral Ezra Justo said sadly. "Even if Marion was taken up by a space vortex he's probably dead. His golden shield was damaged and he would never survive the full power of a space vortex."

"I don't know about that, brother," Admiral Aaron Justo contradicted. "Marion isn't like any other young man I've ever met. He has intelligence and goodness, a rare combination. He can play the ship's harmonic drive like no one I've seen. I think he'll make it. In fact, I know he will."

A ray of hope filled Ezra's heart. He paused just long enough to feel the power of his brother's words sinking in. "I think you're right, Aaron; if anyone could survive, it's Marion. Mark this location for a future rescue. We won't come back alone. If it's war they want, its war they'll get. Prepare for full evasive action. Full harmonic power, now!" he ordered.

* * * * * * * * * *

"It's good to see you sleep so comfortably," the robot remarked as Marion slowly opened his eyes. He looked around and saw the golden navigator standing next to the utility room, connected to the power cord. "I have not had a charge for several days. It is good to have my batteries fully charged again."

"How long have I been asleep?" Marion asked, still a little groggy.

"About 10 hours, sir."

Captain Justo sat up in his chair and looked around at the bowls in the vortex drive. Everything seemed to be in perfect condition. But his mind was fuzzy; there was so much to think about, so much to ponder. He thought about his experience in the space vortex and wondered if it were real. Then he thought back to the events of the torpedo explosion, the attacking Seratians, and breach of the ship's hull. A hundred questions filled his mind.

"Is my father safe?" he asked excitedly. "Have we reestablished contact with the Argo?"

"One question at a time," the golden robot said, almost chastising the human. "I will answer your inquiries sequentially. Question one: Your father has been safe in heaven, as your people call it, for the last three terramonths. He was a fine captain. One of the best I have ever had the honor to sail with. Question two: I do not know anything about a star ship called the Argo, except for one in the planning stages."

"What are you talking about?" Marion asked with frustration. "I was just talking to my father. He commanded us to abandon ship and rendezvous with the Argo."

"Ah, another intrigue? I don't find this one to be very amusing. We were captured by Seratian pirates, barely escaped being destroyed, and you have the nerve to joke about whether your father is dead or alive. Marion Thomas Justo, you are the most difficult captain I have ever worked with."

"Marion Thomas Justo? Is that who you think I am?"

Into the River of Fire

"Captain Marion Thomas Justo is who you are, although last week you claimed to be the Sultan of Rutland."

Marion paused for a moment trying to get a grasp on the situation. Marion Thomas Justo would be his grandfather. How could the robot confuse him with someone 40 years from the past? He decided to try to gather more information.

"So if I were Captain Marion Thomas Justo, who would my father be?"

"Very amusing, I am sure," the robot answered stiffly and went on with his work. When Marion made no indication of backing down, the robot stopped what he was doing and answered the question. "You come from a long and distinguished line of starship captains. I have worked with each and every one of them. Your father, Admiral Lorenzo Justo, was the best I had ever worked with, with the exception of Admiral Albert Justo, the first space vortex captain. I know it is still a shock to have him gone and that you have been thrust into a position you are not ready for, but ready or not, this duty belongs to you."

"One more question, please," Marion asked cautiously. "I don't mean to seem coy or funny. I must have hit my head or something, but I need to know. Who are you?"

"I will answer your question only because your stress levels are extremely high and I note a potential lack of full memory function; but I assure you, if this is another prank I will be most displeased. I am a Cybertronic Humanoid, Series 2450, programmed to navigate between star systems... but you may call me Boom."

"That will be all, Boom," Captain Justo said quietly. "You have saved my life today and I am grateful. I'll be in my quarters just off the command center if you need me."

"Yes, thank you, Captain."

Marion left the vortex drive room and hurried to the command center, deep in thought. It was as though his navigator was stuck in another time. Justo wondered if 40 years ago Boom had sneaked into the vortex drive room after the ship was captured and activated the vortex drive from the utility room. That would have been a fairly clever maneuver and it would explain why the escape pods had been full of pirates. Still he wondered, as he walked to his quarters, what had happened to Cenric, and to Sevan, the king's son. Upon entering his quarters, he gave in to the feeling of complete exhaustion his experience had given him. In spite of his 10 hours of sleep, Marion fell into his bed and dreamt of lightning and spinning vortices of fire.

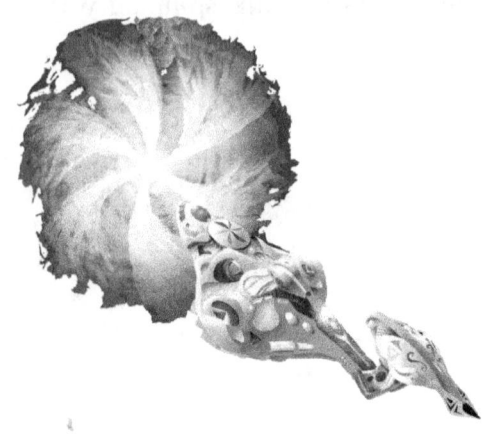

A New World

The ship was sailing totally blind. Not a single star, nebula, or galaxy matched with any chart in the navi-computer's memory banks. Marion and Boom checked and rechecked the accuracy of the computer's navigational systems but, each time, the system completed the analysis perfectly.

The breach to the ship's hull was minimal; it only took 200 pounds of fine gold and two weeks to make the repairs. Luckily, the ship carried reserves for just such a disaster. The exterior rooms connected to the hull had sealed off, as they were designed to do, preventing any further damage to the rest of the ship. Only two rooms were completely destroyed, while a third received minor damage. For now, interior repairs would have to wait; all they could do was close the doors for the time being. Just to be sure the repair was sound, Boom suggested they minimize, to test the ship's integrity.

"That is a good suggestion," Captain Justo agreed. "How small will this ship go? To a scale of 50 or 60 percent of normal size?"

"The Isian is capable of minimizing to a scale of as little as .05 percent of normal, sir," Boom stated.

"You must be mistaken," Marion gasped. "You must mean a scale of 50 percent rather than .05 percent of normal. Point zero five would minimize us to the size of an office desk."

"Precisely, sir, to the size of an office desk."

"No ship can get close to that, not even the Argo."

"Your ghost ship, the Argo, must not be crafted to the design specifications of the Isian, sir," Boom said, rather proudly. "If you are going to make up a ship, at least make it a powerful one."

"I'm not going to get into another discussion about your sense of reality," Captain Justo retorted. "If this ship can minimize to a scale of .05 percent of normal, I want to see it done."

"As you wish. Prepare for an initial 50 percent minimization, then we will take her down from there."

Captain Justo sat in his command chair and brought up his instrument panel from inside the floor of the ship. "Activate minimization protection." As he issued the command, the chair emitted a blue field of energy around him.

"Begin minimizing sequence. Take her down to a scale of 50 percent on my mark. Three, two, one... minimize."

Boom blasted a thousand commands from his chest and both sets of crystal bowls in the vortex drive control room burst into song. The ship glowed a florescent green inside and out and then, in an instant, the whole room changed color turning to a blood-red hue. The sound from the crystal bowls penetrated every molecule of Captain Justo's body while a bright white light flashed around him. As suddenly as it started, it was over.

"Minimizing complete," Boom stated.

"Check the integrity of the repair job," Captain Justo commanded. "I spent two weeks welding out there. I want to know if it all held together."

A New World

"It looks good, Captain," Boom confirmed. "Your work is excellent. We seem to have perfect integrity. Permission to minimize to 25 percent?"

"Permission granted."

Once again Boom communicated with the crystal vortex drive, and again the green and red lights permeated their bodies before ending with one blast of white light.

"Twenty-five percent of normal reached; the integrity of the ship is intact. Permission to minimize the ship to 10 percent?"

Captain Justo agreed to the request, recognizing they were getting very close to reaching the limits of minimization. Marion knew that if a crystal was held in one's hand and thought of as the nucleus of an atom, the nearest electron would be 40 terra-miles away. Even minimizing the ship to 10 percent of normal size still put the nearest electron four miles away. Several more flashes of hot light permeated his body, but he and Boom still remained intact.

"Permission to minimize to five percent?" Boom asked confidently.

"I don't think that's a good idea. Even the Argo can't minimize to five percent."

"I thought you wished to test the minimizing capacity, to discover whether this ship is superior to the Argo or not. Permission to minimize to five percent."

"Now I know why they stopped making mechanical navigators," Marion said exasperated. "You're all insane. Fine, take her down to five percent."

Captain Justo held on to his chair and listened as Boom calmly commanded the ship to minimize to five percent of normal. He felt the blast of heat coming from the vortex drives. Green then red and fiery hot white light permeated everything once again. The ship groaned and shuddered, but followed the sequence, reducing them safely to five percent of normal size.

"Permission to minimize below five percent not granted," Captain Justo yelled before Boom could even ask the question. "We'll perform our tests minimized at a scale of five percent and then we'll maximize back to our normal size. Is that clear?"

"Yes, Captain," Boom said obediently. "Now you can say you have done something even your ghost ship couldn't do."

"Just do your tests," Marion snapped and stepped out of the command chair to wash the sweat off his face. "Crazy robot."

A New World

* * * * * * * * * *

Several days passed before they were ready to attempt their first planned space vortex voyage. After the last voyage he'd experienced, Marion was nervous. But taking control of his fear, he identified a star system 30 light years away which appeared to be located in the correct position and size to be a terra class planet.

All terra-class planets were located in exactly the same orbit around a sun of a similar magnitude. If they were positioned any closer to the sun, the intense heat would boil and evaporate any surface water, leaving the planet a lifeless desert; if they were located any farther away the waters would freeze, creating an endless winter. Each terra-planet had the same tilt to allow for seasons, as well as a single moon to influence tides and more subtle weather patterns. A terra-class planet would have active tectonic plates that would create mountains and valleys necessary for the semi-even distribution of rain and snow, along with volcanic activity to bring minerals and gases from the center of the earth up to the surface. All of this was required for a planet to create and maintain an atmosphere suitable to sustain life.

With such a delicate balance required, many thought it was impossible to find another terra-planet. But as the Isians began to explore the outer reaches of space they discovered millions of such planets, some in early stages of development and others teeming with animal life. Some planets were covered in dense jungle with swamps inhabited by large bird-like reptiles. Other planets were inhabited by large hairy mammals along with violent near-human creatures unapproachable because of their war-like natures. The Royal Republic of Is, as the government was known, forbade any contact with these inhuman creatures.

As the Isians explored their own spiral galaxy they discovered humans living on terra-worlds millions of light years apart who shared common languages and interests despite the distance. Different races were soon revealed as the Isians mapped and charted the interconnected system of space vortices. Pale white skin complemented by light hair was not the only DNA possibility in the human genome. Many other skin types were revealed: brown, bronze, black, yellow, and red, for example. Even though their outward appearance was different, their DNA sequencing was nearly the same. Some races were large in stature and some were small. Some civilizations were very primitive but some were quite advanced.

The Seratian civilization was one of the last civilizations to be discovered and, so far, they were the most advanced. They did not appreciate competition from their newly-arrived rivals. Seratians had already developed sophisticated space travel, but still hadn't reached the level of space vortex travel. It was during this time of transition that Admiral Lorenzo Justo had made contact with the King of the Seratians, encouraging him to study to become an Isian captain, but his mission apparently failed.

Now Marion Justo hoped he would be able to encounter an advanced civilization friendly enough to help him return to his own universe. Boom had scanned every frequency for intelligent life, but none had shown any promise. All they could do was physically explore the river-like path of the space vortex.

They locked in on a star system and Captain Justo gave the command to close all blast shields.

"Blast shields closed, sir," Boom said. Several minutes passed but Captain Justo hadn't given the command to activate the space vortex drive. Boom started to get impatient. "We are ready to activate the space vortex drive, sir; do I have your command?"

"Just wait a minute," Marion said uncomfortably. "You don't have to experience what I do inside the space vortex. After what happened last time, I want to make sure I am prepared."

Portal Four

"My apologies," Boom said politely, "ready to activate on your command, whenever that may be."

Several more terra-minutes passed before the captain sat up in his chair and faced forward. He took a deep breath and gave his command, "Activate vortex drive on my mark. Three, two, one,...activate."

Clear musical tones reverberated from within the mechanisms of the robot and the ship responded by activating the huge crystal bowls along both trailing wings of the starship. Harmonic tones vibrated through every molecule of the ship and the hull glowed with a deep blue and purple. A twirling mass of fire engulfed the entire ship, bringing it into the center of a spinning river of intelligence. Protected by the golden hull of the ship, Captain Justo couldn't see the individual fiery flames surround the ship; nor could he feel the full effects of the green and red arcs of radiating light.

Captain Justo closed his eyes, letting out his last breath. Upon opening his eyes he found the room was lit from within by a gently glowing light. He felt his heart stop, but only for a moment. Before the blood had a chance to stop pulsing, he felt his entire body fill with strength - his lungs full with oxygen. Protected from the full effects of the river of intelligence by his repaired golden starship, he was prepared to enjoy the voyage in the space vortex.

After only a few moments the unearthly lights illuminating the ship dimmed and the Captain's heart skipped a beat, and then began thumping along rhythmically. He was mortal again; the voyage in the space vortex was over. Boom sprang into life and another series of notes exploded from his chest.

"Preparing for full shut down of the vortex drive," he said as though nothing had happened. Through thousands of voyages, Boom had never experienced, really experienced, a single one of them, not being human.

"Open blast shields," Captain Justo commanded.

Now the two explorers focused their instruments on the surrounding star system and searched for signs of life on the terra-planet. And, to their relief, they found a planet full of animal life. As he explored, the captain found that some of the life-forms were very different from what he had ever seen before, with many of the mammals bearing their young live, then keeping them protected in pouches for several more months. Marion recorded everything he could for future scientific study, then plotted their voyage to the next star system.

Portal Four

This pattern of exploration continued day after day, month after month. Some star systems contained terra-planets, some did not. Of the hundreds of living planets they found no human life. Some planets had massive reptiles, others had birds, and still others, dangerous near-humans frightening even to observe. After six terra-months Marion was exhausted and found himself feeling that they would never find another human soul. How would they ever find a way out of this massive and complex star system?

On one such frustrating day, they charted their course for a cluster of stars. Upon coming out of the space vortex they found themselves surrounded by intelligent radio and microwave transmissions.

"We've finally done it," Captain Justo said, excited and relieved. "We've found semi-advanced human activity. Where is it coming from?"

Boom scanned the horizon and located the source of all the life readings; there was a terra-planet only one star system away. He intercepted the fragmented signals, then started running a standard first contact diagnostic. The amount of data was enormous but the ship's sophisticated storage system easily interpreted the mass of information. In a matter of terra-seconds Marion had an initial report.

A New World

"Look at this!" Captain Justo exclaimed in disbelief. "They are communicating in thousands of different languages. I detect 20 or so major dialects, but look at their range. There are Greek, Latin, Germanic, and Isian derivatives, all on the same small continent. Hundreds of dialects of Chinese, Japanese, and other oriental-based languages are bunched together on another continent. And here's African, Hebrew and Arabic all mixed together with Isian. Separated from the rest of the continents are two large continents with a Latin-based language on the southern hemisphere and an Isian derivative occupying the northern hemisphere. Do you know what this means?"

"No one can understand anyone?" Boom responded dryly.

"This must be a violent people. They haven't been in the age of electricity for more than 100 years," Captain Justo said, astonished. "If they had entered it any sooner, their languages would have already homogenized. Check the computer and see if I'm right."

A few bursts of sound came from Boom's chest and the computer flashed a historical account of the planet according to the information transmissions it had been able to garner over the last few terra-minutes.

Portal Four

"It's just as I thought," Captain Justo said, amazed as the data screen flashed images of wars, destructions, and incredible worldwide conflicts. The imager stopped on a huge explosion rising up like a mushroom cloud.

"They used atomics on their enemies," Boom added in disbelief. "What kind of people are these? Never in the history of all humanity, as we know it, has one people used such a barbaric weapon on an enemy."

"Look at this," Captain Justo said, even more astonished. "In 100 terra-years they progressed from animal-drawn transportation to regular scheduled space flights. This civilization is on the fastest development track I have ever seen."

"The fast track to self-destruction you mean," said Boom. "Look at these pollution readings. They've been burning their natural resources at an alarming rate. Whole areas have been deforested. I advise we avoid this planet and seek out another. It's too dangerous."

"There are real dangers," the Captain agreed, "but we should investigate further."

"You have shown real improvement over the last months, sir, but I fear you are resorting to your reckless ways. Please reconsider this decision."

A New World

"I have to find someone and bring him back to our universe," Captain Justo explained. "I can't run away from every terra-planet just because it might be dangerous."

"I don't understand this mission," Boom argued, "but obviously I cannot change your mind, so let us get this over with as quickly as possible. All I can say is your father, Captain Lorenzo Justo, would be very displeased."

"I think my father would approve," Marion smiled. "Prepare for space vortex travel on my mark. Three, two, one, activate..."

Boom and his captain exited the space vortex near the single moon orbiting the shining blue planet. The electronic signals were even more intense than those picked up before. They had originally received transmissions from a star system four light years away, so all the waves they had intercepted were four terra-years old. The computer technology had more than quadrupled in that short time span and the number of transmissions had increased a hundred times. Data was transmitted through huge connected networks and was available to anyone, unrestricted. Ultra-high-frequency wave lengths were sending audio and video text from handheld device to hand-held device. It seemed this world had changed significantly in only four years.

Portal Four

"Permission to leave this terra-planet?" Boom asked.

"No, we can't go. This is the most amazing civilization I have ever seen. There must be five billion people on this one little planet. How do they get along at all? If they are so intelligent, why haven't they figured out ionic energy and started populating the nearby terra-planets?"

"Possibly because they keep killing each other off," Boom surmised.

They circled the planet just on the edge of the moon for several days gathering as much data as they could. Against Boom's wishes, Captain Justo was preparing for a terrestrial visit and had even programmed his communicator to understand the idioms of one of the prominent planetary languages. The language, English, was very similar to Isian mixed with Latin and Greek.

By the third day of observation Captain Justo was getting comfortable with his new surroundings, but he and Boom both agreed to keep their harmonic shield up to full power, just in case the planet had a defense system.

On the fourth day, everything started out calm and serene. The Captain was almost ready to take an escape pod down to investigate the planet at a closer range when the room turned red and the blaring sound of the emergency siren filled the air.

"What's happening?" the captain yelled.

Boom yelled through the clamor, "The main shields are failing. The harmonic shield is losing power!"

"That's impossible," Captain Justo cried.

"Impossible or not, they're failing!"

The young captain frantically entered a few musical chords into his computer and the ear-piercing siren finally was silenced.

"What kind of planetary defense system are they using? I haven't detected any computer software sophisticated enough to even know we are here."

"I am putting the source of the attack on the Comnet," Boom said as he emitted a series of tones from his chest. A loud crashing noise came over the speaker.

"What is that?" Captain Justo shouted over the ruckus.

"I think it may be distorted guitars set to the rhythm of tribal drums," Boom shouted over the loud music.

The music pounded and vibrated the ship causing the seats to rattle. All at once a screeching grating voice wailed over the speaker and spewed profanities through the gilded command center.

"Shut that off," Captain Justo commanded, but the discordant music continued.

"I said turn it off!"

But the music kept playing. Marion looked over to see Boom frantically attempting to turn off the sound but nothing happened.

"I'm unable to shut it off," Boom reported. "I have just attempted two million different commands and been blocked out with every one. Our harmonic shields are completely down, we are losing control of the ship."

"Shut down the communication ports."

"Already tried that, sir."

"What about diverting the signal to a non-essential computer system?"

"Tried that as well and over a million other strategies," Boom affirmed. "Without our harmonic shield to protect us, my only suggestion is to activate the vortex drive and get as far away from this planet as possible while we still have the chance."

"We can't leave," the captain insisted, "this is the only inhabited planet we have come across in six months. We need information. We have to stay."

"Fine, stay," the navigator said sharply. "You are the captain. It's your call whether we live or die, but at least get us far enough away to figure things out... sir, this is bad, our starboard engine has just been infected by a super virus."

The captain stepped out of his command chair and rubbed his temples as if he was trying to squeeze out a little more brain power. For a moment he stood cold and motionless; then a warm grin began to form on his face. He jumped back in his command chair and started opening computer programs.

"They will expect us to move further out," he thought aloud, "so we will move closer in. We'll minimize the ship to its smallest possible size and fly the ship at full speed directly into the planet. In our fully minimized condition we could land on solid rock and still come out unharmed. If this ship can really minimize to .05, right now is the time to do it. Prepare for a crash landing. Minimize on my mark... three, two, one, minimize."

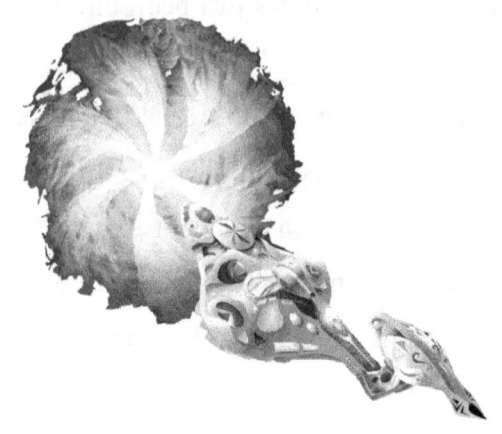

Gold From the Sky

Four hundred thousand miles away from where the Isian struggled for survival, the sun raised its head over the cool mountain skyline on the Earth below. The day started out like any other morning in the early 21st century, with computers turning on for e-mail and cell phones buzzing with billions of conversations. As advanced as computers were getting, cars and trucks were still driving with their wheels firmly on the ground. Intergalactic space travel was centuries away, but for the Sterling's it was as close as a phone call.

"Ye're in grave danger," the voice said, trembling over the upstairs telephone line. "Don't leave yer house until the golden sun has set in the west. If ye're attacked use the blaster I gave ya. Do ya still have it?"

"No," Christopher stuttered. "Is this Uncle Cenric?"

"O course it's me," he chided, "Do ya have the blaster or no?"

"I already said no," Christopher replied. "Daniel thought it was a digital music player and took it to school and lost it."

"Cursed bad luck," he said desperately. "It could've saved ya. Beware! Today there be gold fallin' from the sky. Blast it all. Here it comes again. Take that, ya mangy dog!"

"There's gold where?" Christopher asked into the phone with a confused look. But the phone line went dead without any other information.

"What was that all about?" Amber, Christopher's older sister, asked while she finished putting on her eyeliner.

"It was Uncle Cenric giving us another danger alert," Christopher said while he put the phone back on the receiver. "He wanted to talk to Dad, but since he's in California right now, I said he could talk to Mom, but instead he just left a message."

"So what's the message?" Amber asked impatiently.

"He says we are in grave danger," Christopher laughed, "and that we shouldn't leave the house all day, and to beware of gold falling from the sky."

"Do you think we should tell Mom?" Christopher's little brother Daniel butted in. "It sounds serious."

"Go ahead." Christopher laughed as he started going down the stairs to get some breakfast. "I'll tell her you lost the digital music player Uncle Cenric gave me. He said as long as I had that with me I'd be fine and now look..."

"I didn't mean to lose it," Daniel said defensively. "I think it fell out of my bag and -"

"Chill out," Christopher chided him. "I hated every song on that stupid thing. He's always saying stuff like that. Besides, he's not even our real uncle. Dad's an orphan."

"Well, if you were an orphan, you would be happy for any kind of brother," Amber yelled as Christopher walked out of sight. "At least he got to choose who he calls a brother. I got stuck with you two!"

Daniel stuck his tongue out at her and tried to run back to his own bedroom, but she was too fast and wrestled him back into the main upstairs bathroom, grabbing him by the belt and starting to comb his hair.

"I'll comb my own hair," Daniel complained, struggling with his older sister for control of the comb. "Just leave me alone and let me do it myself!"

"It's no great pleasure for me either," Amber snapped as she let him grab the comb out of her hands. "I'll just tell Mom you wouldn't let me help you and then see what happens."

Daniel thought about it for a second, then sat next to his sister in a slumped position. "Oh, fine, you do it then," he whined, giving her back the comb. "But be more careful. Besides, it's just going to stick straight up anyway."

Amber knew he was right. Daniel's hair was like a blonde wire brush that did whatever it wanted. No amount of water could tame it. In fact, very little could tame any part of Daniel. He was all frogs and sunshine.

At 10 years old, Daniel was short for his age—just four-foot-two—and he weighed in at about 80 pounds soaking wet. His short blond hair never stayed combed and his freckled face never stayed clean. His ears had grown slightly faster than the rest of him, so they poked out a little too far from his head, giving him an impish appearance that made him look consistently guilty. To make matters worse, he had a bad temper with a short fuse. Hardly a day went by without a fight or argument at school.

"Ouch!" Daniel grimaced, trying again to get away from Amber. "Are you done yet?"

"Almost," she declared firmly as she tightened her hold around his shoulders.

"There, I'm done, you wart, now go finish your breakfast, but don't get your shirt dirty. Remember, everything you have on is new and if you get any of it dirty, you're dead."

"Dead shamed," he taunted her.

Breaking free from her grip he ran as fast as he could to the stairs which opened up to the foyer of the old house. The Sterling home was a turn-of-the-century Victorian mansion, originally built by the chief accountant of the Tintic Silver Mines in 1898. At the time, it was the city of Salt Creek's loveliest home. But, unfortunately, years of neglect caused by the falling fortunes of the town reduced the old mansion to a faded, paint-chipped wreck.

When Daniel's parents, Stephen and Edna Sterling, saw the old house, they sensed some of its former glory in the tall ceilings and woodwork and decided to try and keep her alive. All Daniel could see was drafty rooms with creaky floors, along with tall windows that made his friends afraid to come and spend the night.

He ran down the steep stairs, twirling around the corner so fast he nearly dove head first into his older brother's chest.

"Watch where you're going," Christopher growled as he headed towards the kitchen table, a bowl of cold cereal in his hand he was trying hard not to spill.

Fourteen-year-old Christopher was four years older than Daniel. He had a light complexion and blond hair sometimes parted in the middle. He was a little short for his age, too; but at five-foot-five he was catching up and had finally breached the 110-pound mark. He had poor eyesight but wore a pair of handsome gold-rimmed glasses to compensate for it. He was more level-headed than Daniel, but that didn't mean he couldn't be provoked. Sometimes his little brother drove him so crazy their mom had to separate them for what seemed like hours.

Christopher was especially irritated on this particular morning because of his desire to get to church early. Church had always been important to him, but he was even more motivated to attend now since he discovered where all the good-looking girls spent their

Sundays. If he got to church early enough he might even get to talk to Nancy Cloward.

Mrs. Sterling assured Daniel that Christopher's recent grumpiness had something to do with hormones, promising him it would pass someday. At least, that was her hope. Daniel tried to remember that happy thought as he ran into the kitchen to pour himself some cereal too.

"I caught a fish yesterday," Daniel finally said after settling in on a bowl full of corn flakes. "It was a foot long."

"Yeah, right," Christopher challenged. "Salt Creek doesn't have anything but minnows. And if you did catch a fish you probably used Dad's fishing pole without his permission. So, where is this fish?"

"When I took the hook out of its mouth it wriggled out of my hands and got away, but it was a foot long. And I put Dad's pole back where he told me to."

Christopher was crunching down on his cold cereal, trying to decide what kind of cereal he wanted for seconds. He didn't care if he made his little brother irritated. He was older and more mature, which put him above trying to make Daniel happy... so, he laughed out loud.

"So what you're saying is you *almost* caught a fish. That's funny."

"No it's not," Daniel insisted. "I caught it. I had it in my hands. It's just like you said: if you touch it first, it's yours."

"I don't care if you touched it, I don't believe you. I didn't see it, so I don't believe it."

Daniel's temper was about to explode like a dome of molten lava when he heard heavy footsteps coming down the stairs.

"What's going on down here?" Mrs. Sterling said sternly. "I can hear you yelling all the way upstairs."

"He started it," Christopher instinctively responded as if he had rehearsed the line a million times.

"Mom," Daniel moaned, "he doesn't believe I caught a fish yesterday. Make him believe me."

"I can't make him believe you," Mrs. Sterling said as she walked into the kitchen with three small children walking behind her. "But you'd better believe *me*, you were almost grounded for coming home so late."

Christopher smirked, but only for a second. Mrs. Sterling turned her attention to him. "Stop that, son," she said. "If he says he caught a fish then believe him; give him some respect. Sometimes you just have to have faith."

"Here comes another lecture," Christopher groaned out loud.

"Pardon me, young man," Mrs. Sterling said soberly, "this is the Sabbath Day in a Christian household. The last time I checked a mother can still teach her children the Golden Rule in her own home." She shook her head. "On days like this I think I'm raising a bunch of wild goats instead of children. Sometimes it's not what you say that sends the message, but how you say it."

She looked at Christopher with mother laser vision powerful enough to make him squirm.

"What, Mom? I'm listening," he said uncomfortably.

"Be nicer to your brother. That's an order. In a few weeks, when your father gets back from California, we'll all go camping and have some fun. Until then, behave yourselves, okay?"

Both boys nodded their heads weakly as Mrs. Sterling turned and walked back upstairs, the three youngest still following after her to finish getting ready for church.

Mrs. Edna Sterling was the mother of two boys and five girls. Christopher and Daniel, her only boys, were rowdy enough to make her feel like she had five boys and a lion in the basement. On any given day she planned for a trip to the emergency room or a call to meet with the principal in his office.

Of her seven children, Amber was the oldest. She was sixteen, independent, smart, and very outspoken. While Christopher was the oldest boy, Bethany was the next oldest girl. An even-tempered 12-year-old redhead, she was studious, bright, and the main babysitter in the house. Eva was eight, just a year and a half younger than Daniel, and his polar opposite. She had dark brown hair and a sensitive and caring nature. Hannah, at six, was altogether her own person with strong leadership abilities already. The baby of the family, Katie May, was barely four years old. She had a winning smile and could make friends with anyone.

With seven children, Mrs. Sterling had her hands full. She felt like a full-time housekeeper, cook, daycare provider, and prize fighter manager. Her husband, Stephen Sterling, was almost always away on business. Edna, then, was nearly a single mom, making her job doubly difficult.

Currently, Stephen was in California trying to get two different, heavy-equipment computers to talk to each other and it wasn't going very well. Modern machinery was all computer-automated these days, but manufacturers failed to take into account their inability to work independent of other pieces of equipment; so Stephen's job entailed getting everything to work together. Mrs. Sterling wished she could get her own boys to work together a little better as well.

"I did catch the fish," Daniel whispered defiantly.

"In your dreams," Christopher shot back, flicking a wet spoon at Daniel's shirt. A twirling speck of milk floated in the air. Daniel watched in horror as it landed on the pocket of his new shirt.

He glared at his older, bigger, heavier, stronger brother. His anger was too hot to express, at least not without a fight, and he knew he couldn't win.

"I caught that fish once and I can do it again!"

With that, he jumped up and ran out, slamming the door. Running to the garage for his dad's fishing pole, he was soon off to the river.

Through the iron pipe gate and down the old concrete sidewalk... it was only 15 minutes before they had to leave for church, but Daniel didn't care. He didn't want to go to church anymore... all he wanted was to catch a fish and shove the slimy scales up his brother's nose.

"I'll show him," he said to himself as he ran the half block to where the road crossed over the river. He chose a trail, one of many that darted into a muddy bog-like field, then dropped down into his favorite fishing hole.

Almost instantly, peace surrounded him. The cottonwood trees didn't care about arguments and battles; they ignored age, height, and weight. All they knew was the age-old language of water, sky, and light.

"I wish I could live here," Daniel said out loud, wiping a tear from his eye. "No one makes fun of me out here."

He threw a rock into the water, watching it bounce then sink into the river depths. After a while he sat on his favorite fishing log, readying his pole for the hunt. When it was properly rigged, he reached under the log for his secret stash of cheese bait, fixed the bait on the hook, and threw it into the water with a gentle cast.

Slowly, he drew the hook back to see if a fish had taken the bait, but no such luck. He looked into the pool for what seemed to be forever, not thinking of anything, only feeling sorry for himself.

"Life stinks," he muttered. "I'm short, I'm dumb, and my dad can't even make enough money to make our stupid little house payment without leaving us alone while he goes to California."

He didn't budge even when he heard the honk of his mother's Suburban's horn. As far as he was concerned his new religion was fishing. Just as he was about to cast his hook into the water again, something shiny in the tree above him caught his attention.

"What is that?" he said, raising his eyes almost into the morning sun. The car honked long and hard, distracting him for a second, but the shiny object got bigger and bigger as it streaked quickly towards him.

* * * * * * * * *

"Stabilize that harmonic engine," Captain Justo demanded above the blaring of the emergency sirens aboard the shrunken spaceship. Even with his acceleration protection in place, he knew the crash landing would take a heavy toll on his body. Already his head was aching and his stomach felt ready to throw up everything he had eaten for the last three days.

"I have the port vortex drive stabilized," Boom reported, "but the starboard drive is completely out of control. I don't know how long I can keep it from self-destructing. I'm losing control..."

Marion held his temples with his hand, trying to think how to save the infected engine. Suddenly he moved from the acceleration protection of the seat and began entering data into the computer keyboard.

"I'm shutting down the infected starboard engine, and then we'll bring up the ionic backup engines to take its place."

Boom blurted, "The minute you disengage the starboard engine we'll crash! If we survive the crash when the ionic engines come on line we'll be out of balance again, soaring who knows how high. After a few more seconds the two engines will fight for control and we'll crash again!"

"And after a few ups and downs we'll stabilize and have control of the ship," Captain Justo absent-mindedly answered as he continued working on his plan. "I don't think the Argo could handle a maneuver like this, but the Isian might be able to."

"Do not think to flatter me about the Isian's capabilities," Boom retorted. "This is too much even for the Isian. Don't do this."

"I'm sorry," the young captain said calmly as he finished entering his last command, "but it's already done. Get the two engines to work together as quickly as possible. Even with acceleration protection, I'll probably be too motion-sick to help."

Portal Five

Trying to steady his stomach nausea, Marion ordered the computer, "Activate starboard drive shut-down sequence and initiate ionic emergency engine start-up on my mark... three, two, one, mark!"

* * * * * * * * *

If it had fallen from the sky like a rock or fluttered gently down like a bird, Daniel wouldn't have been so startled but, instead, the shiny object came crashing through the cottonwood trees like a meteorite, then stopped dead-still in the air. It hovered motionlessly over the water as Daniel hopped around to avoid being hit by falling tree limbs and branches.

For three long seconds Daniel studied the object's features as it wiggled about like a fish on a line. He could see it was about the size of an office desk, but shaped rather like a stingray with a fat stomach. Its tail rose up elegantly in the shape of a flat violin and strange sounds came from inside the craft; lights flashed all over it - making it look like a Christmas tree with Independence Day fireworks going off inside. And, the most impressive thing about the ship? It appeared to be made of gold.

Daniel was stunned. He inched closer to his log to get a better look, then suddenly the object zoomed back into the air and came straight down, crashing sideways into the shallow depths of the river. The water parted violently, sending a giant tsunami of mud and water toward the helpless boy, reaching out like a claw, crashing over him.

Daniel flew backward several feet from the force of the water and landed in the mud with his freshly-pressed white shirt, suit coat, tie, and new wool pants completely drenched. Picking himself up, the boy ran to the river's edge to get another glimpse of the strange craft. He wasn't thinking about Sunday School or fish anymore, *that* was for sure.

Meanwhile, back at the Sterling home, Christopher reached over to honk the car horn again.

"Stop that right now!" Mrs. Sterling said impatiently, shuffling the little girls into the car. "Bethany, are you here?"

Bethany said, "Yeah, Mom," as Amber opened the passenger side of the large, family-friendly, gas hog of a car, hopping into her assigned seat.

"Now, where's your brother?" Mrs. Sterling sighed, exasperated.

"He's gone fishing, Mom," Christopher said as innocently as he could. "That's why I was honking the horn."

Mrs. Sterling glared at him, her temper starting to rise.

"You egged him on, didn't you?" she raged, finally exploding. "Even when I told you to stop harassing him, you didn't stop, did you? I've had enough out of you, son! You go get your brother from the river, apologize to him, and bring him back to the car. Do you understand?"

"Yes, Mamma," Christopher muttered as he exited the car and slowly walked towards the river.

After a few minutes of searching, he found Daniel staring into the water. Christopher was too far away to notice the water seeping back into the river or the blanket of leaves and tree limbs all around. All he could see was his pain-in-the-neck little brother fishing on Sunday.

"Let's go, Daniel," he said sourly. "Mom and Amber are waiting in the car. I don't want to be late either. You're not supposed to be near the water before church anyway. You can catch your fish tomorrow."

Daniel didn't move... he was too shocked to remember how. Christopher walked closer.

"I said, let's go now!'"

"Look right down there," Daniel exclaimed excitedly, pointing into the muddy bottoms. "Do you see it?"

"I don't see anything," Christopher said without a glance at the water. "It's probably a minnow. Now, let's go!"

Christopher stomped toward his brother and grabbed his jacket to drag him to the car, now noticing Daniel was soaking wet. Just as he was about to yell at him the shiny object suddenly burst out of the water like a missile, sending another wave of water crashing, this time, over both boys.

Stunned, Christopher let go of Daniel's coat. The river water flooded over him, spun him around in the mud, and pushed him head first into the river, as Daniel fell backwards on his rear-end in the mud on the riverbank. Christopher stood up as fast as he could; his new suit was dripping wet.

"What was that?" he yelled... and would have said more, but the craft violently crashed back into the water, sending another avalanche of water and mud at them. The out-of-control vessel surged out of the river one more time and smashed into the upper branches of the cottonwood trees.

It rose and buzzed through a branch that held a heavy rope swing. The branch was eight inches thick but the ship cut through it like a chainsaw before it went out of sight. Suspended in midair for a moment, the branch came crashing down like a falling brick wall and hit the ground between the two boys. Green leaves and dead branches exploded from it as it hit and bounced on the ground.

Before the leaves had even finished fluttering, the unidentified falling object came streaking back (at what seemed like the speed of light), stopped in midair, and hovered six inches over the muddy river.

"I d-don't think it's a f-fish," 10-year-old Daniel stammered.

Covered from head to toe with slimy, stagnant river mud - hundreds of leaves and twigs were stuck in the mud too - along with tree bark that had exploded from the rope swing branch, he looked like a bedraggled swamp monster.

Christopher looked the same, sitting in the shallow river with water up to his waist. His glasses were caked with grit and mud, but miraculously they had remained on his face. Without getting up, he dipped them in the water and tried to get them clean. "Stay where you are, Daniel," he said with his heart nearly pounding out of his chest. "I want to get a better look at this thing."

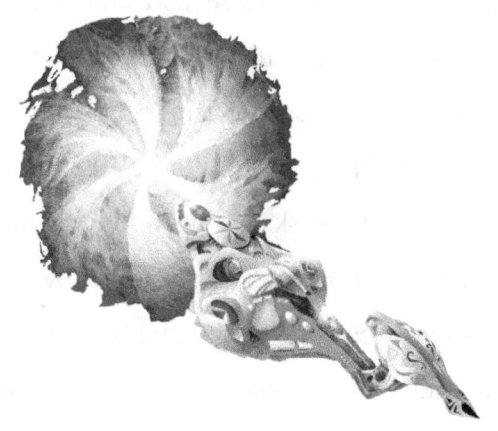

Golden Punishments

Christopher attempted to stand up in the water, but his hands sank into the muddy goop and it was difficult to pull them out. Finally though, he got himself free, his arms looking like elbow-length mud gloves. He stood up facing the ship, and just as he was about to catch his breath, the UFO began belching steam from somewhere inside. Mud dripped off the golden hull, revealing the finely-crafted workmanship. And, even though the ship wasn't moving, the boy could tell something was going on inside.

"What do you think it is?" Daniel asked, creeping slowly to the edge of the water.

"It's some kind of spaceship," Christopher answered confidently. Of course he didn't know for sure, but he wanted to pretend he did.

The ship was about four feet long, with a wing span almost as wide. It didn't look like it belonged in the air but rather like it should be skimming over the ocean like a stingray. The front of the ship was rounded like a clam and gracefully swept backward to the stubby wings, while the back of the wings curved inward towards the body of the ship. The tail section rose from the horizontal plane of the golden craft, towering over it by a foot. It hung over the rear of the ship like a violin ready to be played by its master. However, the most striking thing was the color. The longer Christopher looked at it, the more he was convinced the ship was made of gold—pure gold.

His imagination ran wild, thinking about what he could buy with a wheelbarrow full of gold... houses, cars, and people to drive them, motorcycles and jet skis, skateboards and new clothes. His mind raced as he thought about treasure and everything treasure could provide.

Material dreams were interrupted by a new round of steam hissing and bursting from the odd, golden ship.

"What do you think it's doing?" Daniel asked, squinting into the water to get a better look.

"I don't know," Christopher responded greedily. "But it's mine. I found it first."

Daniel's face froze in a frown. "What do you mean it's yours?" he said, glaring at his brother. Jumping into the water, new shoes and all, he marched towards the ship.

"The rule has always been whoever sees it first, gets it. I saw it first!" His fears were gone. His brother might be four years older and a full foot taller, but he wasn't giving up without a fight. As Daniel approached the ship Christopher grabbed his arm and started holding him back.

Suddenly, the ship began making ringing noises... subtle at first, then gradually becoming louder.

"It sounds like music or something," Daniel declared, hoping to break free of his bigger sibling. Christopher scoffed and held Daniel even tighter.

"It sounds like it's broken to me. Now get out of my way... it's mine!"

The boys struggled, yanking each other back and forth; but Christopher was heavier by thirty pounds and finally got the upper hand, pushing Daniel back into the mud.

Christopher moved forward and reached out for the UFO when the sound of a more menacing threat broke through the trees.

Portal Six

"Christopher Sterling," Mrs. Sterling called sternly. "Where are you? I told you to get Daniel, not to join him. If you two make me late for church again, I'll ground you both for a week."

Christopher was first to respond to his mother's voice, quickly pulling his outstretched hand closer to his body, then suddenly noticing his muddy clothes.

"I don't think Mom's going to like this," he whispered.

The Sterling family only bought new church clothes once a year, and that event had taken place the day before. He felt his colorful silk tie... now caked with slimy mud. His $100 suit was dripping with moss and stinky river sludge and his new shoes were submerged in two feet of water. He started to panic.

Daniel didn't pay any attention. He didn't feel any remorse whatsoever for destroying $300 worth of clothing. He took the opportunity to stand up and start wading waist-deep into the water towards the ship.

"Let *me* touch it," he insisted. "I told you. I found it first."

"Are you crazy?" Christopher yelled. "Mom's coming. When she sees us like this she'll kill us."

"I don't care," Daniel blurted. "She'll see the ship and we won't get into any trouble. She'll be happy I found it for her. I'm gonna make her rich."

"Oh, no you're not!" Christopher blasted. "I'm touching it first you little snot-nosed brat!"

Christopher pulled at Daniel's hand, forcing him under the water. Daniel came up sputtering and gasping for air. Defiantly, he spit a mouth full of river water into Christopher's face then grabbed for the ship. Christopher put his hand in his brother's face, pushing him into the water for a second time. This time he held him down even longer.

Mrs. Sterling could hear her sons' muffled voices, but the underbrush was too thick to see anything, and with each step down the well-worn path her temper escalated. When she finally made it to the open field she paused, listening.

"Where *are* those two boys?" she said hotly under her breath. A moment later she thought she heard Daniel's voice coming from the river bottoms and started walking in that direction.

Mrs. Sterling was normally a pleasant, beautiful woman in her late thirties. She had a petite build and dark brown eyes. Her shiny dark hair hung neatly over her shoulders. Both boys respected her and sometimes even feared her. She ruled the house with stern but fair rules, but when those rules were broken, especially on purpose, the boys knew they were in for some serious consequences.

Mrs. Sterling was already at her wit's end when it came to her children's behavior. For the last week the boys had been bickering and fighting with each other nonstop. Just a few days before, Daniel had picked all the roses off a neighbor's prized bushes. Now this morning's antics were about to become the straw that broke the camel's back. Normally she had her husband around to help hand out the punishments, but the work that had taken him away on business was taking longer than expected. She had to handle all the discipline on her own and it was more than a little overwhelming.

Christopher could sense his mother coming, but he didn't dare let go of his brother who was still thrashing around under the water. Daniel was finally just about to place his finger on the ship when suddenly it whisked silently back into the air and came crashing back down inches from his outstretched fingertips.

But Mrs. Sterling didn't see the ship. Her eyes were focused on picking her way through the weedy rock trail while the trees and change in elevation hid the movements of the golden ship from view. As she walked down into the river bottoms the golden ship streaked silently up into the sky and crashed once again into the flowing river this time sending a newly-created wave of water over her as she entered the secluded area. The poor woman was drenched in slimy river mud and water... from her feathered hat to her very new white shoes.

Daniel was thrown clear out of the water onto the riverbank. As he gasped for air he didn't notice his equally soaked mother standing a little higher up on the riverbank. Christopher, tossed face-first into the shallow mud near the bank, raised his head and spit out leaves and brownish green slime. Luckily, his glasses, unbroken, were still on his face. After coughing and spitting for a few seconds he regained his composure.

"I told you it was mine," he sputtered. "Now look at what you've done, you moron, you scared it away." He sat in the mud, taking off his glasses to clean them for the second time. Christopher still couldn't see anything in detail, his glasses were too dirty to look through... but what he could see of his mother's condition made his stomach drop like an anvil.

"I think we're in serious trouble," he groaned.

Mrs. Sterling was more than soaking wet; she was making strange gurgling noises. Suddenly she started to cough, spitting out pieces of moss. She reached down and felt the dripping hemline of her best, dry-clean-only dress. With the other hand she found the limp feather on her new hat.

"What in heaven's name!" she screamed, "what in the -"

She stopped yelling to check her limp, wet clothes. Then, turning round and round like she was doing a tango, she lifted her legs up and down like a bird landing on a hot car hood.

"I can't believe this!" she erupted like a volcano. "Look at me! Look at my clothes, my hat, and my shoes!" Then she stopped looking at herself and looked at them.

Christopher was standing knee-deep in sludge. Daniel was sitting on the shore like the prophet Jonah just thrown-up by the whale.

"Look at you!" she screeched all the louder. "You're swimming in a mud hole in your best Sunday clothes. What am I raising, pigs?"

If she said other words, Daniel didn't hear them. He saw her marching towards him and darted away before he could be caught... running desperately all the way home.

Christopher wasn't so lucky. He had to struggle in the mud to get to the shore and by the time he made it, he was met with his mother's hand squarely on his shoulder.

"There's a spaceship in the water, Mom. It was the spaceship that got us wet. I promise."

"Do you expect me to believe that?" Mrs. Sterling stuttered in disbelief.

Too angry to listen to anymore explanations, she didn't wait for an answer. But fortunately for the boy, her hands were still slick from the slimy water and her footing uneven, causing her to stumble a little and her hand to slip from his shoulder. Whatever punishment she had in store for her son would have to wait.

Christopher took the opportunity to break free and ran up the rocky trail to the road above. From there, he too sprinted home as fast as he could.

"How could this be happening to me?" Mrs. Sterling asked out loud, starting to cry. "What do I do now?" She wished with all her heart for her husband. Then the thought of her two disobedient sons came into her mind, bringing fire back into her eyes. As angry as a wet hornet, she turned and made her way back up the road just as Amber was about to run into the woods.

Portal Six

"Mom, you're soaked," she said in horror. "I came as fast as I could after seeing Daniel; then a minute later Christopher ran past me on the road looking like he'd taken a mud bath. What happened?"

"Spaceships," Mrs. Sterling told her seriously, then yelled. "Isn't that obvious? Now go get the car and pick me up. I refuse to walk home looking like this."

Amber didn't question anything. She hurried home and drove the car to where Mrs. Sterling was hiding.

When Christopher got to the house, Daniel was in the backyard taking off his dirty clothes. He passed Amber running from the river, then watched as she jumped into the car and peeled out of the driveway. He knew his mother would show up any moment. Christopher joined Daniel, stripping as fast as he could. He glared at his brother in the meanest way he could, then took off a shoe and threw it at him while he still had the chance.

"Don't worry," he parroted in a nasally voice, "We won't get in trouble, everything will be all right... fat chance of that."

"Fat chance of that," Daniel mimicked defiantly. "Anyway, I found it first. Besides, you nearly drowned me."

"Shut up, Daniel."

"No, you shut up," Daniel insisted, throwing the shoe back.

They were ready to start throwing punches when the Suburban came rolling into the driveway. "Bethany, get the girls in the house," they heard Mrs. Sterling order solemnly. "We're not going to church today."

"We're supposed to be a happy family," Bethany sobbed, shuffling the rest of the crying girls into the house.

"Now we're really dead," Christopher moaned. "Here comes Mom."

The driver's side door of the Suburban slammed shut. Moments later Mrs. Sterling came marching around the corner followed by Amber. She glared at her sons; both instantly put their heads down.

Mrs. Sterling focused her attention on Daniel first. He had most of his clothes off except for his pants, and was squirting his legs with the hose in an attempt to get the mud off without getting too cold. She grabbed the hose from his hands and aimed it directly at his bare chest.

"Turn the water up," she yelled over her shoulder to Amber, who dutifully complied. Water gushed out of the hose and Daniel yelped in surprise at the icy shock.

"I have never been so insulted in my whole life," she barked. "You're both grounded until your father gets back from California, and I mean it!" She squirted the garden hose at Daniel like a fireman putting out a flame. The water pounded on his bare chest and wool pants for several minutes, washing all the dirt away.

Finally he'd had enough.

"I'm clean, I'm clean," he pleaded, "please let me go upstairs and take a shower."

"Go then," she agreed and squirted him one last time on the back. "After that, stay in your room for the rest of the day, and don't come out until breakfast tomorrow."

Daniel raced into the house without turning back to see what was going to happen to his older brother.

"It was a spaceship," Christopher whined pathetically, knowing it was his turn next.

"Just stop!" she yelled. "Don't say another word. Just give me your glasses."

He handed them over as she continued, "You and your brother have been fighting for weeks. I can't believe you would take it to this extreme, and on a Sunday! A water fight in your Sunday clothes and you drag me into it. If you want me to play in your water fight, I'll play."

She walked over to the side of the house and turned the water on even higher, adjusting the spray nozzle to hard.

Christopher knew he was going to get it, and there was nothing he could do to stop it.

"I'm telling the truth," he sputtered getting a face full of garden-hose water.

"I said, don't talk until I'm done." She took the hose and aimed it directly at his shirt. Mud flew everywhere, spattering the ground. She forced him to turn around several times until every piece of his clothing was cleaned. With his clothes cleaned off, she forced him to take off his shirt and shoes and socks, everything except his pants, and sprayed him down until he nearly turned blue.

"Now you go upstairs and get yourself showered," she finally said, more subdued. "When you've done that, sit in your room for the rest of the day. Do you understand?"

"Y-yes M-mother," Christopher chattered and ran into the house as fast as he could.

Bethany was looking out the window with her other sisters and Amber stood by the Suburban with her arms folded.

"Can I turn the water off now?" she asked quietly.

Mrs. Sterling held the water hose for a few more seconds, then began to cry. Amber didn't wait to be told. She hurried over to turn off the water, then gathered up the filthy suits and shirts.

Portal Six

"What am I going to tell your father?" Edna Sterling sobbed. "How do I explain all this money wasted?"

Amber didn't know how to answer. Instead she took all the clothes that could be washed and started a load of laundry. The other clothes she hung on hangers, setting them out to dry. Their mother walked numbly up to her room and closed the door, all the while crying quietly.

After his shower, Christopher got dressed in warm clothes and sulked on his bed. He looked over at his brother, but Daniel wouldn't take the blankets off his head. In the distance he could hear his mother cry. No matter how he positioned his pillow or turned his head he could still hear her sobbing. His heart felt sick. He hated to hear his mother cry. Still, he knew what he had seen and no amount of punishment or guilt could take that away.

* * * * * * * * *

Neither Daniel nor Christopher disobeyed their mother's orders for the rest the day. They stayed in their room and didn't dare say anything. Though the two boys shared a room, a wall of silence separated them.

The day went by very slowly, with neither boy daring to talk for fear of upsetting their mother. Missing lunch and dinner was a heavy punishment, but complete

Golden Punishments

silence turned into the perfect situation for Christopher to make a plan.

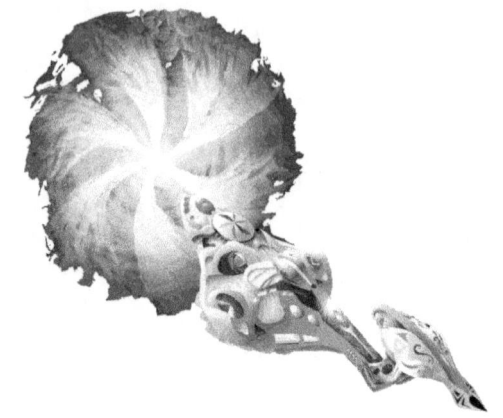

Sunken Treasure

Christopher rolled over to look at the clock. It blinked back at him in red digital letters. "It's still only 3 a.m.," he groaned to himself. "If only morning would come faster."

His stomach growled for the five hundredth time. Even school lunch was starting to sound good. He looked over at his brother sleeping like a rock.

"If only I could sleep like that," he said quietly to himself.

As he admired his brother's sleeping abilities, a blue light began to glow from Daniel's sleeping eyes. Seconds later Daniel's hands morphed into two razor-sharp knives. The blankets that had covered him were cut into pieces by the pincers as he sat up in his bed. His feet became heavy metal hooves that moved with lightning speed and crashed to the floor. By the time he stood up his whole body had transformed into a metallic monster - only his face remained human, with the exception of the blue light blazing from his eye sockets.

"You wanted to touch it first," Daniel spoke in a buzzing garbled tone, "touch it now." From behind the bed the spaceship rose above his mutated brother and hovered menacingly in the air.

"Touch it," the monster demanded. "Touch the spaceship and become like me!"

The ship inched closer and closer until Christopher fell off his bed in a blind panic, ran into the closet, and closed the door. All at once the door flew off its hinges, breaking into shredded pieces. The monster slashed a huge hole in the wall, making room for the space ship to enter the closet.

"No, no," Christopher screamed. "I won't touch it. Leave me alone." The ship sped right toward his chest. He thrust his hands forward to protect himself from the impact, screaming with all of his might.

He woke in a cold sweat.

"Are you all right?" Daniel asked, jumping over to his brother's bed. "You scared the heck out of me."

"It was only a dream?" Christopher sighed. "I thought you were trying to kill me."

"That would be a switch, wouldn't it?" Daniel smirked. "While we get dressed, tell me all about it."

For the next 10 minutes Christopher gave a play-by-play account of his nightmare. When he finished they crept downstairs to get some breakfast. Corn flakes and toast tasted great after a 24-hour fast and a long, sleepless night. Just as Christopher was about to go into more details of his dream, Amber and Bethany came down the stairs and entered the kitchen.

"Did you sleep all right?" Amber asked Christopher snidely. "Yeah," Christopher replied without looking up from his second bowl of cereal.

"Oh." She sighed, "I could have sworn I heard you screaming at the top of your lungs.... 'No, stay way, I won't touch it.'"

She smiled, pouring herself a bowl of cereal. "Are those little green men getting to you?"

"Just shut up… I don't care what you think. I know what I saw and you're not going to change that."

"Be nice to each other," Bethany pleaded. "Mom said to stop fighting."

She would have said more, but at that instant her mother came walking into the room.

"What's going on here?" she asked sternly.

"Nothing, Mom," Christopher said, as innocently as he could. "There's nothing going on, just breakfast, right Daniel?"

"Sure," Daniel agreed. "Just breakfast... and it's really good, too. Thanks for everything, Mom."

The room went silent. Amber didn't dare say anything while Bethany just kept eating her breakfast.

Finally, Christopher broke the silence. "I'm sorry about the clothes," he said in a near-whisper. "I'm sorry about your dress too and everything else... really I am."

Then Daniel added his apology. "I didn't mean to get wet; it just all happened so fast. I'm so sorry." He nearly fell out of his chair as he gave his Mom a hug.

Mrs. Sterling stood for a few seconds, finally letting out her breath and smiling weakly.

"I really don't know what to do with you two." She sighed. "I was prepared for the terrible twos, but I'm not so sure I'll survive the horrible teens."

She was still upset about the destruction of her new dress and hat, but she loved her two sons too much to be angry forever. Mrs. Sterling had already gathered up all the suits, shirts, and ties in hopes the dry cleaners could salvage them, but she had little hope for her hat.

"I want both of you home right after school," she said sternly. "And if you even *think* about going near that mud hole, I'll send you both to military boarding school. Is that clear?"

They both nodded in complete obedience. Christopher ducked into the bathroom just before they were about to go to school to grab something without his mother noticing. Daniel saw him but didn't dare ask what he was doing.

Neither boy talked as they left the house, walking with Bethany to the end of the street where she happily said her goodbyes and skipped away to her best friend's house. Though she went to the same school as Christopher, she never walked with him any farther than Missy's. The other school-age girls, Eva and Hannah, attended the same grade school as Daniel, but they started at a different time, since it was next to impossible for their mom to get all seven children off to school at the same time. With Bethany safely out of sight, Daniel finally broke the silence.

"I know you, Christopher," Daniel said soberly, "you have a plan, and I bet it's going to get me into a lot of trouble."

"It could," Christopher agreed, "but we have to take the chance." He didn't say anything else all the way to school. Obviously in deep thought, Christopher had an intense look in his eyes like he was planning the heist of the century. Daniel didn't dare disturb him. When they reached the school flagpole where Christopher normally dropped off his little brother, he broke the silence.

"Listen," he said earnestly, "I want you to meet me here as soon as school is over, you understand?"

"Yeah, sure," Daniel agreed. "What are we going to do?"

"I can't tell you right now. Just meet me here."

"Okay," Daniel agreed reluctantly. "See ya then."

Christopher turned around without saying goodbye, heading quickly toward the junior high, leaving Daniel standing in a complete daze. He briefly considered skipping school and going to the river by himself, but after the trouble he'd been in the last time he sloughed, he decided against it. Besides, he didn't want to ruin anything his brother had planned.

He walked slowly into the school and occupied his seat. Sitting in his seat was about all he could do with his mind churning in so many different directions. The rest of the day was the same... he couldn't concentrate. He looked at the clock so often it felt like his neck was going to permanently stick in that direction.

Finally, by the end of the day, his mind had started to thaw out a bit, and he could do simple tasks like paying attention to a full sentence and raising his hand while pretending to look interested.

At last it came - the ringing of the final bell. Daniel treated it like the starting gun of a great race and jumped out of his seat, tearing out the door. He darted down the hall, out the double doors, and ran for the flagpole. To his delight, Christopher was already there, huffing and puffing. It was obvious he had run all the way from the junior high.

"Let me catch my breath for a second," Christopher whispered, panting. "After that we'll run all the way to the swimming hole."

"We're not supposed to go to the swimming hole," Daniel objected, trying to convince his brother he wanted to be obedient. "You know what Mom said at breakfast this morning. Do you like military food?"

Christopher frowned. "I heard her loud and clear. That's why we have to run all the way there, look for the UFO, and then get home before she knows we're missing. Are you ready?"

"I'm ready," Daniel complained. "But I'm also getting ready for military school. By the way, what did you put in your backpack this morning?"

"I've got our swimming suits, towels, dad's goggles, his snorkel, and a bag of chocolate chips," he said while shifting the contents of the backpack getting ready for another hard run.

"What are the chocolate chips for?"

"To eat," Christopher said, looking at Daniel like he was a goof ball. "Come on, we don't have any time to waste."

The two boys ran about two blocks, then stopped for a few seconds to catch their breath, still a half-mile from their destination. By eastern standards the river wasn't much of a river. It was a stream really, but it flowed all year round; to a westerner in a desert, it was a full-fledged river.

After the boys caught their breath, they crossed Track Street, ran another block, then made a right hand turn on Center Street. They had to be careful because their house was on Center Street. Now, sneaking past the intersection, they ran to 100 South without stopping. About to take a short cut through Mrs. Seastrand's backyard, they heard footsteps coming up behind them. It was Benny Strong, the meanest kid in town.

"Where are you two girls running off to so fast?" Benny taunted. "I bet you're running to pick a fight with me, aren't you?"

Christopher didn't want to answer the bully. Benny was bigger and meaner, but mostly he was just in the way. Every moment was precious that afternoon and Christopher didn't want to waste a single minute.

"Don't talk to him," Christopher whispered, begging his brother. "Just ignore him; maybe he'll get tired of running and go away."

Daniel wasn't afraid of Benny, so he didn't understand his brother's reasons for keeping quiet. "We're not afraid of you," Daniel blurted. "Just leave us alone."

Benny was the youngest of three boys. He was a year older than Christopher, but in the same grade. He'd been held back for flunking too many classes in seventh grade, but that suited Benny just fine. It made him that much bigger and more able to beat up the younger boys. He also lacked adult supervision. His mother worked 12-hour days at the local hospital and his father had left the state a few years earlier after a bitter divorce; he hadn't paid a penny in child support since. Benny could pretty well do whatever he wanted; he was completely free. Unfortunately, his only pleasure was making every other kid in town just as miserable as he was.

Benny caught up to Daniel and started poking him. "Oh, so you're not afraid of me?" he said tauntingly. "Well come on, I haven't had a fight all day."

"Leave him alone," Christopher mumbled, feeling his heart jump up in his throat.

"Did you say something?" Benny sneered. "I didn't even know you could talk." He ran faster now and caught up to Christopher, giving him a hard shove. Christopher flew to the ground, taking Daniel with him. In the tumble the goggles fell out of the backpack and slid on the gravel.

"That's better," he laughed. "Now you look like the dirt bags you are."

Benny walked over to where Christopher was trying to get up and grabbed his shirt. "This will teach you to back talk me," Benny said as he gave him a solid jab to the stomach. Christopher fell back to the ground gasping for air, the wind knocked out of him.

Benny walked around Christopher's panting body laughing, then noticed the goggles. "I'll take these as payment for crossing me," Benny announced. He fumbled around with the goggles, trying to figure out how to put them on.

"Give those back!" Daniel yelled, jumping up to grab them.

Benny fought back and pushed him into the dirt. "I'm tired of you, midget," Benny screamed. "It's time that I teach you some manners. No, I think it's time to beat the crap out of you."

Benny swung his fist to hit Daniel in the mouth when Christopher jumped him from behind, ripping the goggles from his hands.

"Run, Daniel!" he yelled.

He didn't have to say that twice! Daniel grabbed a handful of sandy dirt and threw it in Benny's eyes. Without taking another look he got up and ran after his brother as fast as he could.

"I can't believe you did that," Daniel yelled as they cut through Mrs. Seastrand's backyard. "Hanging around you has rotted my brain cells," Christopher said as he panted.

"Anyway, I think we lost him."

They crossed the field and walked to the river. It hadn't changed a bit.

They were about to break into the backpack when Benny yelled from the road. "I know where you're going an' when I catch up with you I'm gonna break your stinkin' heads open."

"I thought we lost him," Daniel said, panicked.

"So did I. I bet he's on his bike. Let's get out of here."

The only place to hide was the bog, a muddy stand of rushes and cattails 20 feet or so from the swimming hole. Because of its smelly, pasty mud, the bog was strictly off limits. But off limits or not, the bog was the only safe place to go.

The brothers darted for it in a mad rush.

Christopher was able to run to safety without getting too muddy, but Daniel didn't have the same luck. He picked a bad spot to cross and soon was up to his ankles in stinky mud. He struggled for a second, then in one huge effort his feet popped out of both shoes; one shoe flipped onto firmer ground and the other was lost in the bog.

"I just lost my shoes," Daniel whispered loudly.

"Well then, go back and get them," Christopher ordered, knowing he was safely hidden; he wasn't going to move an inch.

Daniel ran back barefooted and tried to pull the shoe out of the mud. "It's stuck," he yelled.

"Shut up!" Christopher demanded, "get the shoe later. Here comes Benny." Daniel quickly ducked down and hid himself in the rushes. Benny raced into the field on his bicycle and rode around wildly.

"I know you're hiding around here somewhere," he yelled. "When I catch you, you'll be sorry you were born." He got off his bike and started to look around.

When he couldn't find the two brothers, he got even more annoyed. Just then a red blinking light caught his attention. He walked to the edge of the bog and picked up Daniel's shoe.

"Lookie what I found," he said with a sneer, "a doggie bone."

Daniel's heart dropped. His shoes were not just any shoes. They were Action Lights, the coolest shoes ever, with a red light in the sole that lit up with every step. They would have stayed on his feet but he never tied his shoes. It was cooler to just tuck the laces in the tongue. Daniel could hardly contain his despair. He'd put in three months of extra chores to earn those expensive shoes. Now they were gone in a heartbeat, the full loss hitting him like a brick.

"Give me back my shoe. I'll call the police on you if you don't."

"There you are," Benny snarled. "Come out and get it yourself." Benny waited a few seconds.

"I gave you the chance," he lied, "now I'll just have to give this to my pit bull. But don't worry. She'll have it torn into pieces so little even the police won't be able to figure it out."

Benny grinned in pleasure as he heard Daniel crying in the rushes.

"Now let's find the other one," he said loudly. He looked around for a few minutes and then made a loud grunting noise; Christopher could tell he'd found the other one.

"Leave the shoe alone," he ordered, as he revealed his hiding spot. But when he looked to where Benny should have been he was nowhere to be seen.

"This isn't a shoe," Benny said with surprise from some distance away. "What is it?"

Christopher stood up, peeping through the cattails and saw Benny wading in the knee-deep mud, making his way towards a strange light he had mistaken for Daniel's shoe. Christopher's heart sank. Benny made it to the deeper side of the river and stood directly over the light.

"What is that?" he mumbled, peering into the murky water. "Is that what I think it is?" He couldn't get a clear view of it so he took off his shirt, tossed it to the bank, and submerged himself completely under the water.

"It's made of gold," he screamed when he came up. "I can't believe it. I'm a millionaire. I'm rich! I'm rich!"

Christopher walked out of the bog and dropped the goggles on the firm ground. Tears of pain came into his eyes... it was like he'd flushed a winning lotto ticket down the toilet. Daniel noted Christopher's bravery and stopped crying long enough to see what was happening. When he saw and heard Benny screaming with joy and dunking himself in and out of the water he knew their treasure had been discovered.

"Do you think he'll share?" Daniel said wiping the last tears from his eyes."

"Not on your life," Christopher muttered. The boy he feared the most had smashed all of his hopes and dreams.

Benny had uncovered more than half of the craft. It was lying on its side, firmly covered in the mud; but no matter how hard he pulled he couldn't get it to move. He was about to give up and get a rope when the ship suddenly righted itself, popping out of the slimy mud.

"I've got it," the bully hollered, jumping up and down in the water. "I'm rich, I'm rich!"

Daniel finally made it out of the bog, hopping around clumsily as he tried to find a spot to stand without getting his stockinged feet stuck in a sticker patch. He lost his balance and almost fell, grabbing his brother's shirt to stay up.

"Don't touch me," Christopher said spitefully. "This is all your fault. I'm going home now. You can find your own stupid shoes."

Christopher walked out of the bog in complete despair.

Suddenly, somewhere near the river, Benny started to scream in pain. Christopher crept over to the riverbank and peeked over the edge to see what was going on. There was Benny thrashing around in the bog like an alligator was attacking him. The water around the golden space ship bubbled, boiled, and hissed then sent out a cloud of steam that covered the whole riverbed. Benny continued screaming in pain as he tried to work his way towards the shallows, his feet sucking down into the mud. Frantically scrambling to get to the shore, he saw Christopher. "It's trying to kill me," he yelled.

"Grab my hand," Christopher offered, holding out his hand, but Benny refused. He fell on the shore and then tripped on the fallen rope swing branch, and landed face first in its twigs. With blood oozing from a fresh cut on his forehead he crawled out of the branches and ran out of the woods as fast as he could.

Christopher was stunned. A giant cloud of steam filled the whole riverbank. Sprays of water vapor hissed out of the cloud and shot nearly to the tops of the trees. They bubbled and popped like water droplets hitting a hot pancake griddle.

"I'm glad we didn't try that!" Daniel exclaimed.

"You can say that again," Christopher agreed.

Both boys stood like statues.

Several seconds passed before the hissing stopped. The normal sounds of the river came back, as if nothing had even happened. Everything was the same except for the huge cloud of fog and a faint ringing sound in their ears.

A gentle breeze began to move the cloud away and, as the seconds passed slowly, another amazing part of the spaceship was revealed. Within a few minutes the whole craft was came into sight, hovering peacefully above the slow-moving water.

"I'll let you touch it first," Daniel whispered.

But Christopher slowly shook his head no, remembering Benny... he didn't move a muscle.

Portal Eight

Shrunk and Suffocated

Christopher's mind was racing. Maybe it was a NASA experiment gone crazy... or a fallen military satellite with some kind of automated recovery system. He didn't know much about Russian or Chinese technology, but he doubted they could make anything *this* sophisticated.

"It's not a meteor," he said quietly, "and it's not an automated drone. They don't move once they land. This has got to be from outer space."

Just the thought of those words gave him goose bumps all over. After seeing what it had done to Benny, he wasn't about to get any closer to it. Even so, the idea that it wasn't from this world had only just crossed his mind.

Suddenly the ship started to move, floating smoothly off the water, gliding up the bank towards the boys. Christopher's heart started pounding out of control. Daniel was so petrified he barely had a pulse. When the golden ship was crashing in the mud and knocking down tree limbs, it didn't seem so menacing. But now that it seemed to be controlled, it didn't look helpless anymore.

"Christopher, it's moving right toward us!" Daniel yelled.

"Ya think?" Christopher asked. Pretending to be in control, he started backing up slowly. "After what I saw it do to Benny, I think it has a death ray."

"A death ray?" Daniel screamed at the top of a whisper. "You didn't say anything about a death ray this morning."

"Just move back slowly," Christopher advised, his voice trembling. He felt as if he were walking on a tight rope 50 feet in the air with his eyes closed. The golden ship moved forward every time the boys moved backward. It silently cleared the bank and hung three feet in the air above the rocky field.

* * * * * * * * *

Aboard the Isian, Marion Justo was sorting through different-sized space boots. Boom was in the command center, talking to him through the ship's com link. "Now what are you going to do?" Boom asked sarcastically. "Are you really going to minimize two harmless boys?"

Meanwhile, inside the ship, Captain Justo was adjusting his space suit. "That's the plan," he said. "We've already talked about reprogramming the starboard engine, but to do that I need at least one more strand of DNA. Since you don't have DNA, you're no help."

"How are you going to keep them alive without spacesuits?" Boom asked. "As soon as they're minimized the normal oxygen surrounding them will be too thin to do them any good. They will also be scaled to .05 percent of normal size while keeping their mass. They'll sink in the dust as soon as they're minimized."

"I have that all figured out," Captain Justo assured him. "You're going to open the small bay door and let a roomful of condensed air fall on them. I'll have a couple pair of levitation boots with me and will try to get them back in the ship with those before the oxygen runs out."

"So why not capture just one of them, and leave the other alone?"

"I would love to do that," Captain Justo answered, "but they appear to be brothers. I might as well take them both. It'll be trouble to try to separate them."

Shrunk and Suffocated

"How can you tell they're brothers without a DNA test?" Boom said dryly.

"I can tell by the way they argue." Marion smiled. "Only brothers talk to each other like that. Don't worry; I know what I'm doing. Just keep those two engines talking to each other. I don't want to be squashed by an out-of-control spaceship. How is the harmonic shield holding up?"

"It looks good for the moment," admitted Boom. "It appears the attack is over, but I suggest you get this done quickly. There is no guarantee I can keep everything together by myself."

* * * * * * * * *

"This isn't working," Daniel said in terror. "It's after us. Every time we move, *it* moves."

"Shut up or you'll scare it," Christopher begged quietly.

"Scare it?" The younger boy gulped. "Why would it be scared of us? What are we going to do, beat it with a stick?"

"It could be scared. Maybe Benny turned on an automatic defense shield or something. Don't move... maybe it will just fly away."

Portal Eight

"Well, that's just swell," Daniel said bitterly. "I can't move and I'm standing barefoot in a sticker patch. If something bad happens you better come get me."

Just then, the ship let out an earsplitting series of sounds. They seemed to penetrate every molecule of Christopher's brain. He held his ears as if the sound was going to burst right through his head and leave him lying dead on the ground. Then, unexpectedly, the sound stopped and a beam of intense light shot out of the bow of the ship. It started out green, turned to red, and finally became one brilliant, hot white light. It was so hot it felt like his clothes were going to catch on fire.

"We're dead. We're dead!" Daniel screamed and fell backwards into the sticker patch.

The same thing must have happened to Daniel, thought Christopher.

Blinded by the light and nearly deafened by the intense blast of sound, Christopher fell to his knees in anguish and prepared to die.

Then just as suddenly as the sounds stopped, the light was gone too. Everything was completely silent except for the sound of the wind and the distant whimper of his little brother. It took a minute for him to readjust his eyes to regular sunlight, but when the world finally came back into focus, he didn't believe what he saw.

He looked around and noticed that the grass, once under his feet, now came up to his shoulders. Small rocks looked like boulders. Twigs were as big as tree limbs. Everything else was bigger, too. The trees looked like San Francisco skyscrapers and the small Salt Creek looked like the Mississippi River.

Then it struck him. He had shrunk. He was only three inches tall!

"What's going on here? What's happened to me?! Where am I?"

Off in the distance he heard a muted cry, and remembered his little brother.

"Daniel!" he yelled at the top of his lungs. "Where are you? Are you all right?" He listened closely, but all he could hear was Daniel sobbing, and a cold flash of worry swept over him.

He started to make a plan to rescue his brother when something else more urgent drew his attention... he could breathe but no matter how he tried, he felt like he couldn't get a full breath and everything around him started to spin. The world looked strange anyway, but now the trees danced around his head like he was in a dream. About to pass out, he looked up into an airless daze and noticed for the first time that the now huge golden space ship was directly over his head. He felt fear start in his throat but he was too weak to move.

Suddenly from the spaceship an object fell directly towards Christopher - it looked like a giant raindrop. He couldn't do anything to stop it so he just closed his eyes and prepared for a direct hit. After what seemed like an awful eternity the "raindrop" crashed on to his head, slid over his body, and bounced and jiggled all around him.

"I've been hit," Christopher whispered in a daze, "I'm done for." He held his breath until his lungs couldn't hold out any longer... then, finally, he gave up and exhaled, expecting never to breathe again. He resisted for a few more moments, but his body finally took over and forced him to inhale. But instead of the poison he expected, his lungs filled with sweet pure air. He was too weak to smile so he just sat on the ground and took in one mighty breath after another. The lack of oxygen had turned his fingernails purple so the boy decided not to move until the pink returned.

Now, regaining his senses, he started looking at the bubble around him. He put his hand up and touched its border. It moved slightly at his touch, but his hand easily pierced it. The droplet was completely transparent, holding its shape like a drop of water on a rock. He didn't know it, but the droplet was filled with specialized condensed air meant to keep Christopher alive in his shrunken state. And now, with his blood fully charged with oxygen, he could look around and see beyond the droplet. Everything *seemed* the same, except it was all larger than normal.

I've been shrunk, he thought in silent amazement.

He was about to investigate further but his feet kept sinking into the softer than normal ground. He tried to find rocks to stand on but even some of those broke under his weight. Then he heard the faint cry of his brother floating in from far away.

"Daniel!" he called in a panic, "where are you?"

"Christopher?" Daniel sobbed in the distance, "is that you?"

Christopher looked in the direction of the sound and saw Daniel kneeling about 50 feet away, surrounded by the same kind of bubble.

"Stay there!" he yelled, "I'm coming to get you."

He stood on a larger rock and put his hand out of the clear raindrop skin and then slid his arm out as well. Inch by inch, he slithered out of the droplet until he was completely free.

Portal Eight

"I wouldn't do that if I were you," a voice warned him from behind.

"What the heck!" Christopher twirled around to see where the voice had come from and there, standing squarely in front of him, was a human form dressed in what appeared to be golden armor. His pants were shiny, almost white, and a breastplate of gold covered his shirt. The sleeves had chain mail-looking material at the elbows with armor on the biceps and the forearm. Black gloves covered his hands, with gold plating on top of the digits. His feet were shod with thick, solid, metal boots and a brilliant gold helmet enveloped his head completely with a clear glass-like bubble over his face. When Christopher realized what he was seeing, he let out a blood-curdling scream.

"Run for your life, Daniel! It's got me! Run!"

He turned around to run himself, but all his energy had left him, and once again he couldn't breathe. He opened his mouth to pull in the oxygen but the thin air didn't satisfy his need.

"If you leave the air droplet, you can't breathe," the alien said firmly. "Get back in."

"Please don't kill me," Christopher begged in a wispy voice. He couldn't say anything else. He didn't have the strength. With his head spinning the boy turned toward the air droplet and fell into it.

"You'll be all right in a few minutes," the alien said confidently, taking his arm and dragging him fully back inside the bubble.

When Christopher came back to his senses, his eyes focused on what appeared to be a young man sitting on a rock, dressed in golden armor and now holding his space helmet.

"Are you all right?" the alien young man asked earnestly.

Christopher was almost too stunned to respond. He moved away from the warrior, pushing himself to the edge of the droplet.

"Where am I?" Christopher stammered, his eyes as big as pizzas.

"The same place you were when my spaceship shrank you," the young man responded calmly as he shifted his weight on the rock to sit more comfortably.

"That's impossible," Christopher said quietly, "nobody knows how to shrink people. Where am I? What have you done to my little brother?"

"He's still over there," the spaceman said, pointing northeast. "But don't worry, he's safe. You panicked more than he did, although according to the results of my brain scan he won't be so easy to reason with."

"You scanned our brains?"

"I had to," the alien answered calmly. "How else was I going to translate your language? You wouldn't be able to understand a thing I said if I didn't."

Christopher was starting to regain his composure. He looked at the spaceman and really started to notice his human appearance.

The alien didn't look like he descended from an insect... he had blonde hair, blue eyes, and fair white skin. The spacesuit he wore didn't have tubes or wires poking out but instead looked like a modern version of a medieval knight from King Arthur's court. The breastplate had a bright red design of interlocking snowflakes in the center with gold embroidery at the edges. Under the breastplate was a shirt made of tightly-linked mesh that looked like it was made of gold instead of steel. A hood came up over his ears made of the same linked mesh.

But what really caught Christopher's attention were the spaceman's shoes; they appeared to be crafted out of pure gold, with silver laces running up the middle. The soles were thicker than a regular pair of shoes and had lights flashing all along the sides.

Daniel's got to see those shoes, he thought.

Then he remembered what was happening to him and the panic rushed back over him again.

"Please don't kill me," Christopher pleaded. "I'm too young to die."

"Why would you say that?" the knight asked intently. "Is it a common practice to kill boys on this planet?"

The spaceman smiled and then stood up showing his full height of six feet (if not a little taller).

"They don't appear to be hostile," the alien said in a relieved voice to someone Christopher couldn't see. He pushed back his hood and aired out his short blonde hair. "The mind probe seems to have worked perfectly. I'm communicating just fine. Contact me if there are any further emergencies. Captain Justo, out."

"Please don't torture me or suck my brains out," Christopher pleaded again. "I'll tell you anything you want to know about Earth. I promise."

"That's good news," the Captain said. "I don't have time for killing people today. Can you tell me your name?"

"I'm Christopher Sterling," he responded in a mouse-like voice.

Portal Eight

"It's a pleasure to meet you, Christopher Sterling from the planet Earth," the spaceman said boldly. "I am Captain Justo from the planet Is."

Captain Justo stood straight up, bent in a deep bow, held it for a few seconds, then straightened up.

"I apologize for the rude treatment," he continued, "but my ship crashed into your stream over there and we had a terrible time getting out. Did we harm anyone? Did the minimizing hurt?"

"Did the w-what hurt?" Christopher stammered. He couldn't believe he was having a civilized conversation with an extra-terrestrial.

"Did the shrinking process hurt?" Captain Justo asked, trying to rephrase the question so the boy would understand. "The first time is kind of a shock isn't it... but it's not too bad after that."

"Oh, minimize," Christopher finally responded. "It didn't really hurt, but my ears are still ringing. Why did you have to do that?"

"I need to have you come aboard my ship," the Captain said, pointing to the golden craft above them. "It takes a lot less energy to make you small than to maximize my ship and risk further detection. I know this has taken you by surprise, but I need your help. I hope you will come aboard of your own free will, I would hate to have to subdue you."

"Subdue me? Am I being abducted?"

"It's kind of an emergency," the Captain said impatiently. "I mean a real emergency. If you'll come peacefully, it will save a lot of time and potentially a lot of lives."

"So this does mean I'm being abducted," Christopher said in amazement.

The captain thought about it for a second and agreed, "Yes, I am abducting you, but in the most cordial way."

"Cool! Let's go." Christopher grinned for a second... then stopped. "But I'm only going because there are millions of lives at stake. If you're going to make me do anything evil like blow up the Earth or start an alien invasion, then I won't help you do anything."

"No invasion," Justo assured him, "but if we don't get back to my ship in time, *it* will probably blow up and take your whole town with it."

"You're kidding, right?" Christopher stammered.

"No, I'm not," the captain responded seriously. "The other boy is over there. I haven't explained anything to him yet. I think we'd better get to him before he tries to walk out of the oxygen bubble and turns blue like you did."

"Turn blue... I didn't turn blue."

"Don't argue with me," the Captain commanded. "We don't have time. Do exactly what I tell you and, with a little luck, we might all be alive tomorrow. Got it? Now follow me."

"How?" Christopher complained loudly. "I can't even walk without sinking waist-deep in dirt, and if I step outside of this bubble I can't breathe."

"Oh, I forgot, you have to put on a pair of levitation boots!" the Captain exclaimed. He reached into a backpack and pulled out a pair of golden boots.

"Put these on. Levitation boots are always needed after a person has been minimized."

"Will I!" Christopher took off his old tennis shoes and hurriedly put on the golden shoes. Since science was his favorite subject in school, learning about this new technology was really exiting.

"How does minimizing work?" Christopher asked as he fastened the last buckle on the first shoe.

"It's the science of removing empty space between atoms without changing the object's form or weight,"

Captain Justo explained. "Are you done with that boot yet? Do you need -"

"No, I'm fine," Christopher interrupted. "Let me get this straight: I still weigh 110 pounds, even though I'm only three inches tall?"

The Captain smiled. "I guess you could put it that way, but let's try to move a little faster."

"What kind of air am I breathing?" Christopher pondered while fastening a buckle. "Is it some kind of condensed air?"

"That's right," Captain Justo said even more impatiently, "your body has been reduced in size but it still needs the same volume of oxygen it did before. The only way to get it is to breathe condensed oxygen. It's denser than air, so it acts just like a droplet of water. I am only telling you all of this so you'll hurry up. How do they fit?"

"Pretty good," Christopher said, his fear gone.

He couldn't believe it! Just four minutes after meeting a space alien, they were having a friendly conversation. He stood up slowly. His weight pressed down into the shoes, but he didn't sink into the ground. The boots were sturdy, snug, and looked really cool.

Portal Eight

He took several small steps... as he moved forward part of the air droplet moved with him while the shoes slid around a little as if he were walking on rough ice.

"It will take some getting used to," Captain Justo assured him, "but you'll soon get the feel of them. Don't worry about running out of oxygen; the shoes carry a 24-hour supply.

"We have to walk over there and get your friend now," he smiled knowingly. "Just flex your legs and jump. That's the easiest way for a novice to get started."

"He's not my friend," Christopher announced with a touch of annoyance as he flexed his legs and jumped, "he's my brother."

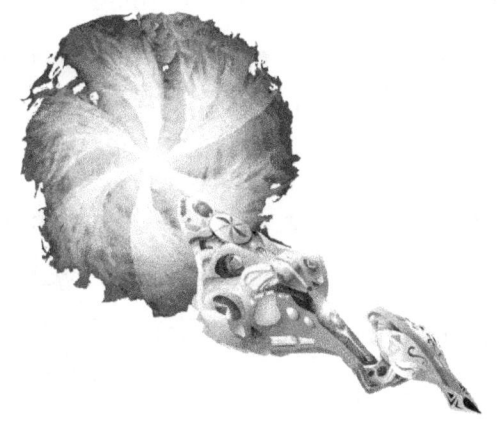

Alien Abduction

With a mighty leap, Christopher soared... in his tiny stature he seemed to be 10 feet above the ground. When he came down to earth his left foot hit the dirt and pushed him back up. It wasn't hard at all to maintain control, but he didn't know how to slow down. With each footstep he flew higher and higher. "How do I stop this thing?" he yelled in a panic.

"Just put your feet together," the alien said, bouncing right along with him, "then lean back and dig your heels into the ground."

Christopher took one more flying leap, then slammed into the ground with both feet as close together as he could get them... but they weren't very close and he lost his balance and lunged forward, toppling over the ground like a tumbleweed on the open prairie. He cart-wheeled over and over until he came to an abrupt stop, right in the arms of his little brother.

"Not bad for your first try," Captain Justo said, while coming to a light landing a few feet away. "And I see you found your brother, too. Well done."

The captain pulled out another pair of levitation boots from the hidden backpack and handed them to Christopher.

"I'll let you deal with your little brother," he said with a smile. "His brain patterns are very aggressive right now and I don't have time for a fight."

Daniel had been practically knocked out of his air droplet by Christopher's crash landing; he started to scream.

"Stay away from me, you imposter," he yelled. "You ate my brother!"

"I *am* your brother, you dope! Now stop screaming," Christopher stated matter-of-factly while brushing the dust off his pants.

"No, you're not," Daniel insisted even louder. "You ate my brother and took his human form, just like in *The Invasion of the Body Snatchers*."

"Stop yelling," Christopher demanded firmly. "You're hurting my ears. Now give it up and put on these shoes."

"I'll never give up," Daniel screamed, hopping to the other end of the air bubble like a wounded bird. He'd already taken his socks off back by the bog, and had very tender feet due to the stickers imbedded in them.

"Stop being a baby," Christopher finally yelled. "You're ticking me off! We're being abducted by aliens, now just put on these stupid shoes before I beat you up."

"I'll never surrender!" Daniel hollered, trying to move away.

"I've got to get back to my ship," Captain Justo interrupted over the confusion inside the droplet. "This is an emergency. If we can't get the shoes on him now, we'll have to leave him down here for a while and come back and get him later."

"No problem," Christopher assured him. "I can get those shoes on. It will be just like getting him ready for Sunday School."

Portal Nine

He grabbed his younger brother by the back of the neck and slammed him to the ground. Daniel resisted, kicking and screaming, but he was helpless as his older brother got him in a head lock.

"Quick!" Christopher yelled. "Get the boots on him before I lose my grip. I can't keep his face pinned to the ground forever."

Captain Justo looked bewildered, but he didn't waste any time putting the levitation boots on Daniel's squirming feet. Kicked in the head more than once, it took all his patience not to leave the boy in the bubble and just take the older one. But a few minutes later both boots were on the boy's feet, despite his boisterous objections, and they were ready to go.

"I hope your Sunday School didn't teach you that," Captain Justo said, struggling with the last boot clasp. Deciding to leave it undone he continued, "There, I've got it. Now let him go and let's levitate to the ship."

"Levitate?" Christopher asked. "How do we levitate?"

"Just stand still and keep your shoes pointed down at all times," Captain Justo answered as a blue beam came down from the open door in the spaceship. Christopher was too enthralled with the thought of levitating to notice his little brother was ready to keep fighting.

"I'll never give up," Daniel screamed, jumping on Christopher's back. At that very moment the levitation beam surrounded them in brilliant blue and white light and the trio started to rise from the ground. Christopher struggled to stay up, having never levitated before, and the extra burden of his dangling brother made it even more difficult. They had already risen to about 50 feet in the air when he started to lose his balance.

Captain Justo tried to help, but Daniel was too persistent. With a desperate tug he pulled his brother off his back and they both started falling.

Pointing his head down, Captain Justo followed the two tumbling boys. He grabbed Christopher's shirt and pulled as hard as he could.

"Get your feet under you," he begged.

"I'm trying," Christopher groaned.

"Convince him you're really his brother or we'll never make it," Captain Justo yelled.

"I can't convince him," Christopher complained. "Daniel's too stubborn to believe anything unless he's hit over the head with it."

Portal Nine

"I don't believe you," Daniel yelled again as his hand slipped a little. Falling a few feet, he grabbed hold of Christopher's leg, squeezing his eyes tight shut. In an attempt to stabilize the two, Captain Justo clutched Christopher by the waist to keep him from toppling over. Finally, Christopher regained his balance by crouching in a wrestling stance.

Once again the three rose steadily to the ship, this time with Daniel firmly attached to his brother's left leg. They floated effortlessly through the open door of the spaceship and rose seven feet up into a brightly lit room; the door shut tightly beneath them as the blue and white light shut off.

Without the power of the levitation beam, all three travelers fell onto the closed bay door in a crumpled pile, with Daniel underneath, still squirming and yelling in a muffled voice. Captain Justo was exhausted from holding them up all the way to the ship. Eventually he rolled out of the pile and stood up with beads of sweat all over his face.

"You two are crazy," he berated the boys. "If I didn't need you so badly I would open the door and let you fall to the ground right now, *without* the levitation beam."

He took a deep breath then continued.

Alien Abduction

"But the fact is, I do need you both and I need you alive, so stop fighting. I have to get the equipment ready for the DNA transfer. Wait here for a few minutes. Can you do that?"

Christopher nodded his head. Daniel didn't respond. He was still attached to Christopher's leg and refused to open his eyes.

"I'll be right back," Captain Justo said as he ran out of the room. Suddenly he ran back and yelled, "And don't touch anything!"

He slammed the door, leaving the two boys alone in the levitation bay.

"I'll never surrender," Daniel whimpered one last time, without letting go of Christopher's leg.

Christopher grabbed his little brother by the head and forced his eyes next to his own. "I'm your brother," he said with gritted teeth. "Open your eyes and let go of my leg. You're hurting me."

Daniel didn't open his eyes. "You're not my brother," he insisted defiantly. "My brother told me he was captured by the aliens. You ate him."

"Open your eyes, you idiot," Christopher said even more agitated. He grabbed Daniel's eyelids and attempted to pry them open. Finally he got one opened and pointed it toward his face.

Daniel looked at him, screaming, "You ate my brother, you're a fake!"

"Oh yeah!" Christopher exploded. "Would a fake brother do this?" He grabbed Daniels nose and twisted it, making Daniel yell in protest.

"Would a fake brother do this?" Christopher asked as he kneaded his fingers into a ball and rubbed them on top of Daniel's head.

"Okay, okay," Daniel finally conceded. "I'll look... I'll look. Just stop hurting me."

Christopher let go and allowed his little brother to get a good look at him. He held out his finger.

"It's me," he said. "Look at this finger." he begged. "Would a fake brother have a scar on his finger? A scar where his stupid little brother almost chopped his finger off while cutting carrots for dinner?"

Daniel's eyes opened wide. He looked at the scar, considered the explanation, and finally accepted this ultimate proof of authenticity. He let out a whooping holler and fell against his brother's unopened arms. "You're alive," he cried. He gave his brother a hug and wouldn't let go.

Christopher accepted the affection for a few seconds before pushing him away. "Don't get too mushy."

"We did it," Daniel yelled as he let go of his brother and began dancing around the room. "We beat those lousy aliens; we sent 'em home runnin'!"

Then he stopped and looked around confused. "Where are we?"

"We're on their spaceship, you moron," Christopher said, amused. "So stop the stupid football dance and sit down. I'm trying to think."

Daniel looked confused. "How can we be on their spaceship? It was only two yards long. How did it get so big?"

"It didn't get big," Christopher informed his brother, his eyes growing comically larger. "We got small. Face it... we've been abducted by aliens."

"Abducted by aliens," Daniel repeated softly. His mind started to slowly take it all in, then a broad smile appeared on his elfish face.

"Sweet. Did you see what they looked like?"

"Yeah, I saw them. You would have seen them too if you weren't acting like such a knot head."

"I thought you were dead," Daniel said sadly. "Anyway, what do the aliens look like?"

"I only saw one," he whispered quietly, trying to create the proper mood. "But it was hideous. It was so horrible I can't even begin to describe it. The only word I can think of is green Jell-O."

"Eww, gross," Daniel responded, pinching his nose. "Does it have extra hands, a green slimy tongue, and red glowing eyes? Stuff like that?"

"Yeah. He looks just like that David guy Amber used to date."

"D-David?" Daniel stammered. "David isn't green. His tongue may be a little slimy but I still liked him. What are you talking about? I thought you were describing a space monster!"

"I am," Christopher continued, "but you're too stubborn to listen to anything."

"I'll listen... just tell me what it looks like."

"It looks like a person," Christopher finally admitted, "a human one. I looked all over for gross stuff, but I couldn't see anything at all."

Daniel's amazement disappeared; he was clearly disappointed. He sat down on the carpeted floor and sulked.

"Great! I get abducted by aliens and I don't even get to see *Star Wars* creatures. I won't have anything exciting to tell my friends. Maybe I'll get to keep the shoes, though," he said attempting to comfort himself.

"Maybe we'll get out of here alive," Christopher mumbled, looking around the strange room for a way to escape if needed.

After a few minutes in the belly of the ship, Christopher's eyes began to adjust to the darker interior. Meanwhile, Daniel was fiddling with his golden shoes, trying to figure out how they worked. But no matter how he jumped, he couldn't make them levitate an inch.

"I think these things are broken," he said.

"I think your head is broken," Christopher shot back as he started looking around the room. "We're inside an alien spaceship and all you can think about is a stupid pair of shoes."

Daniel stopped jumping and started walking in wide circles with his arms out stretched. "These shoes are not stupid," he objected. "Besides, why should I worry? You said he was just a human and not some creepy monster."

"Well, I lied to make you feel better," Christopher responded absently while he continued to look around. "He really has two heads, flipper hands, and a slimy tongue that slithers out of his nose."

"As if that were true," Daniel laughed. "You won't even go in the basement alone if it's dark, so I doubt you'd be so calm if he looked that awesome."

"I ought to deck you," Christopher sneered, "and I go into the basement anytime I want to. Come a little closer and I'll show you a dark room right now!"

Daniel saw Christopher make a tight fist... he decided to stop pushing his luck.

"All I know is that I think this place looks stupid."

"Stupid?" Christopher repeated. "What are you talking about? You haven't even looked around to see anything. You don't even *know* what this place looks like."

"Yeah, I have," Daniel responded blandly. "It looks like a stuffy old museum. I don't think we're even in a spaceship. I think some grandma sucked us into her big old parlor. The only cool thing I see are these shoes," he said trying to jump again. "If only I could make them work..."

Christopher looked at his brother, rolling his eyes. "You are such an idiot."

He did have a point, though. The room was about the same size as a large living room parlor with a ceiling about 13 feet high and a big flat crystal chandelier hanging in the center. It didn't have any windows, but it did have several doors. Christopher hadn't been brave enough to get close to one because the captain told him not to touch anything.

Daniel really had made another point Christopher had to admit was true... at least to himself. He didn't like dark basements *or* dark closets, or anything creepy for that matter. Sometimes he didn't even like being alone in the house during the day. He wanted to walk into a dark room bravely and not search for a light switch, but the unknown held terrors for him. But one thing he did know was that he didn't like his snotty little brother laughing at him about it.

Daniel stopped walking in circles and now tried to walk up the wall. Christopher gave him a sour look and turned in the other direction. It was apparent the walls were too fancy to be a sidewalk; the baseboards were beautifully carved and there was flowered wallpaper and white chair moldings. Above the moldings was smooth pink plaster that rose to the top of the wall. The room had paintings of mountain scenes and people dressed in elegant yet simple clothing standing in forests or sitting on wicker furniture. The frames were ornately carved, carefully crafted with beautiful lines of gold and silver. Christopher couldn't get over the beauty of the paintings.

What a strange transporter room, he thought.

Portal Nine

He wondered where the blue light had come from, but all he could see was the chandelier, held in place by a large, fancy wooden circle. The ceiling's frescos were like those of an ancient cathedral, like the scenes from the Sistine Chapel painted by Michelangelo. He'd seen them in a book once, except these people and cherubs were completely clothed in sweeping robes. Christopher walked backwards, admiring the art. Then all of a sudden he tripped and fell to the floor.

"Hey, watch where you're going," Daniel complained, as he sat on the carpet pulling stickers out of his feet; flecks of mud and dirt were all over the floor.

"You watch where you're sitting," Christopher said sourly. "And look at the mess you're making with all that mud. What are you doing that for?"

"Because I have stickers poking into my feet," Daniel answered angrily, "so just leave me alone. I'm trying to survive here."

Christopher plopped down next to his little brother without saying a word, but Daniel scooted away and continued to clean his feet. Several minutes passed without either boy saying anything.

Daniel, feet finally free of stickers, put his shoes back on.

"I'm sorry for yelling at you," Christopher finally said softly.

"Are you sorry for smashing my face into the ground, too?"

"Yes, I'm sorry for that, too," Christopher admitted. After a few more minutes of silence Daniel cheered up a little and tried to think of something nice to say.

"Well," he whispered, "I'm sorry for pinching and scratching your leg. I thought you were dead."

"I wasn't," Christopher said softly.

"I know that now, but I thought you were. I was afraid."

Both boys sat together in the middle of the room without saying a word, lost in their own thoughts. After a few more minutes Daniel began to squirm. He tried to get comfortable, but after a few seconds he moved again, changing from a crossed-leg position to kneeling.

"What's wrong now?" Christopher asked, slightly annoyed.

Daniel shifted to another position and then reluctantly responded. "I have to go to the bathroom."

Christopher half-laughed and half-scoffed.

"You have to go to the bathroom? Are you crazy?"

"It's not my fault," Daniel said as he stood up. "I had four cartons of milk with my lunch today."

"Four cartons of milk?" Christopher asked in disbelief. "Did you beg for milk from everyone in the lunch room?"

"Not everyone, only from my friends. They hate milk and I like it. Only now I have to pee and I don't think the aliens would like it if I did it in a corner."

"That's great," Christopher complained with his arms folded. "You're just going to have to hold it."

"I have been holding it," Daniel said annoyed. "I don't think I can hold it any longer. You're going to have to call someone or show me where I can go."

"You want me to ask?" Christopher said in disbelief. "Why should I ask? You're the one with the bladder problem."

"Because you're the big brother," Daniel whined as he started holding himself and dancing around nervously. "Please, Christopher! Please, oh please!"

Christopher looked mildly disgusted, but then... he liked seeing his smart-mouthed little brother looking so uncomfortable; he really didn't want to do anything about it.

"Please!" Daniel begged again, this time even more desperately. "You talked to him. You know him. Help me this one time, please," he pleaded.

"Fine," Christopher finally agreed. "Just stop begging. It drives me crazy."

He walked slowly toward the door, his hands starting to sweat and his breath coming in shallow puffs. After what seemed like an eternity he made it to the door and timidly put his hand on the door handle. He held the handle frozen in fear.

"Open it," Daniel yelled. "Hurry!"

Christopher glared at Daniel, then slowly opened the door. "Captain," he called timidly, "I need to talk to you."

Daniel looked at him with his head tilted sideways. "Do you call that a yell? I'm going to pee my pants here."

Christopher got his courage together and yelled as loud as he could. "Captain, we need you!"

Daniel looked at his brother with a big smile.

Christopher poked his head through the open door, looked down a long hall, then quickly closed the door. His heart beating like the wings of a bee, he stood with his head against the wall, trying to calm down.

A few minutes later the young captain came running down the hall with a pair of small tweezers in one hand and a headset in the other.

"So you're both still alive?" he asked hastily, fumbling with his headset. "That's good. I thought you were calling me in here to order a stretcher or apply first aid or something."

Captain Justo looked at Daniel's strange behavior. A look of concern swept over his face.

"Is he really hurt?" he asked. "He looks like he's in pain."

Christopher tried to put his request into words, but he didn't know exactly how to do it. "He ah... He needs a... ah...."

The captain looked at Daniel again and smiled. "Oh, I see," he said. "Follow me."

The captain walked down the hall with the boys, pointing to a closed door.

"The facilities are right here, but don't go into any other room and don't touch anything. I'll come get you in a few minutes. I'm almost ready for you."

With that, Justo ran back down the hall. "I'm coming, I'm coming," he said responding to an unheard, unseen crew member, and disappearing up a flight of stairs.

"What do we do now?" Daniel asked, still squirming in pain.

"I guess we open the door and let you do your thing," Christopher responded. "But be quick, and don't get the seat wet."

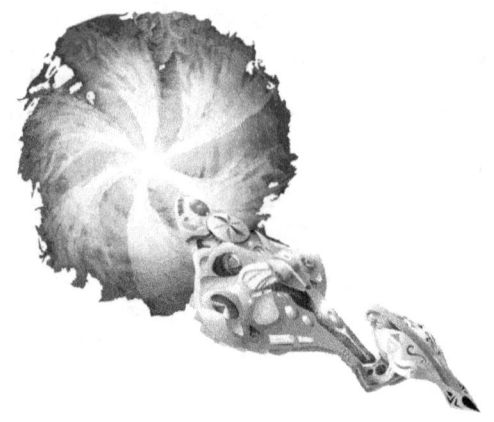

Eerie Tentacles

Daniel slowly turned the door handle and walked nervously into the alien bathroom. When he saw the toilet, he quickly closed the door. Christopher only saw into the room for a few seconds, but he didn't see a single thing he didn't recognize.

Daniel opened the door a few minutes later with a relieved look on his face. As he started to walk out of the room a woman's voice called out to him, "Please flush the toilet."

"Did you say that?" Daniel asked, looking around at Christopher.

"I didn't say anything; the voice came from in there."

"Please flush the toilet," it said again, this time more firmly.

They both walked into the room and looked around for the source of the voice, but they couldn't find it. Christopher walked next to the toilet and pushed down on a small lever. The water made a swishing sound, emptied into a hole somewhere in the bottom, and quickly filled back up again.

"Indoor plumbing?" Christopher smirked, turning to Daniel to complain, "I swear this is all a joke. What kind of spaceship is this anyway? Where are the automatic doors? Where are the robots running around doing stuff? I haven't seen a single plastic part on this whole ship. Even the toilet seat is made of wood."

Daniel reached for the seat and carefully put it down. "Thank you," the toilet said in the same female voice. Daniel jumped back a little.

"The doors don't open by themselves," Christopher continued, "and the toilet doesn't even automatically flush. What kind of place is this?"

"The bathroom talks," Daniel said eagerly. "That's kind of cool."

"Oh yeah," Christopher griped, "that's what I want, a computer to watch me take a leak. Hey, computer. What do you have to say for yourself?"

The mirror above the sink lit up and an image of a woman in her fifties appeared in the glass. Her face was cold and stern. With a notebook in her hand she started to read.

"The unidentified 10-year-old male has an over-abundance of insulin in his system, caused by the consumption of too much chocolate. I recommend green vegetables in his next meal and very little sugar for the next few days to counterbalance the high level of insulin in his blood stream. I will have a full report sent to the meal replicators to prepare a proper balanced diet. End of report."

The mirror went dark and the two boys looked at each other amazed.

"You have an over-abundance of sugar in your system?" Christopher said sharply. "Now I have proof that you've been stealing my Snickers."

They both walked out of the bathroom and closed the door. They didn't want to hear the computer complaining about it all the way back to the transporter room.

"That's the meanest toilet I've ever seen," Daniel stated.

"What do we do now?" Christopher pondered out loud, his curiosity getting the best of him. The talking toilet was kind of cool, and he wondered what other mysteries were hidden behind closed doors.

"We'd better get back to the transporter room, Christopher."

"We'll get there," Christopher said in a sing-song voice, "but first I want to check out what's behind a few of these doors."

Daniel didn't object too much. After all, his brother was the boss and if they got into trouble he knew who to blame.

Christopher walked up to a door and opened it slowly. His heart started beating faster again; he couldn't believe what he was doing. The dark interior was slowly illuminated until its contents were clearly visible. Daniel started to laugh. Inside the room was a sink, a rack full of dust rags, brooms, and squirt bottles full of what appeared to be cleaning supplies.

"Congratulations," Daniel jibed. "You've just discovered a janitor closet."

Portal Ten

Christopher scowled at Daniel, closing the door. Walking over a few feet, he opened another door. Feeling much braver this time, he peeked in, but he couldn't see anything. He walked into the totally dark room and suddenly the door closed behind him.

He turned around, trying to find the door, but he couldn't see anything. The whole room started to spin and his chest contracted in shallow breaths as he started to panic. He tried to scream, but his vocal cords had stopped working. Just as he was about to fall over with fright a blinding light came on. Christopher spun around in terror only to find Daniel with his hand on a light switch.

"There it is," Daniel said cheerfully. "I knew I would find a light switch around here somewhere."

"I ought to deck you," Christopher said, exasperated yet relieved. He would have said more, but his eyes caught the spectacular view of the room. "Now this is more like it," he grinned approvingly.

"I've never seen anything like this before," Daniel agreed.

The lights illuminated a room full of hundreds of crystal bowls—the largest were as big as two hot tubs side by side, 6 feet deep and 20 feet across. The next bowl, only slightly smaller, fit partly inside the biggest bowl, like they were on a rack ready to be washed in a dishwasher. The next bowl, only slightly smaller, fit together in the same fashion. They continued getting smaller until, at the end of the line, the bowl was no bigger than a thimble.

Their sizes were not the only wonder. Only part of the glass containers were exposed; the other part lay hidden in a wooden case, no doubt for protection. Each bowl was held up by a sophisticated mechanism hung from the wooden case so each bowl could turn independently of any of the others.

"It's like that weird instrument Benjamin Franklin invented," Christopher thought out loud.

"What instrument?" Daniel asked.

"You know," he continued. "The Armonica. It was a wine-cup-instrument that you played like a piano. Don't you remember? You sat down like you were going to play the piano but instead you touched the rims of the crystals and they made a really eerie ringing sound. It sounded just like that," he said, pointing to the one bowl that was making a lot of noise.

"I've never heard of it," Daniel admitted.

"Yes, you have," Christopher insisted. "Maybe you haven't seen Benjamin Franklin's instrument, but one that does the same thing. Almost every Christmas we get our fingers wet and rub the rims of our crystal glasses. You remember... after a few seconds it starts making that ringing sound."

"You're right," Daniel exclaimed. "It *does* sound like that. It drives Dad crazy when we do it. But why would you have a room full of crystal in a spaceship?"

"I don't know," Christopher admitted. "But do you hear that sound? It sounds just like the weird music we heard when we first found the ship."

Daniel tilted his head, listening carefully. "I've heard it all along, but I didn't know where it was coming from. I think you're right. This one is making all kinds of sound."

Christopher walked over to where Daniel was standing. He could hear the singing sound of the glass.

"It's ringing, just like you said," Daniel said. "I can hear it singing." Daniel noted another bowl making more music than all the others. He stood in front of it, marveling at its beauty.

"I wonder how it feels," Daniel said, his hand already outstretched.

"Don't touch it," Christopher yelled, but too late... Daniel had already put his hand on it.

Within a split second the floor below them dropped. The two boys flew in the air, almost hitting the ceiling. Gravity started to bring them back down but the ship lunged upward beneath them and they crashed into the floor with kneecap-smashing velocity. After the first vicious jolt the ship continued moving and shaking violently.

Almost instantaneously the whole ship went on alert. Alarms blared, white lights changed to brilliant red. The cups all started singing wildly, the sound so loud it hurt the boys' ears. The ship rocked back and forth like a tug boat in a typhoon, and each time they lost their balance they had to touch another crystal bowl to keep from running into it. With each cup they touched the instability of the ship got worse.

"Stop touching the crystals!" a voice demanded from behind them. "I told you not to touch anything. Especially not the crystal bowls!" Captain Justo stood outside the door of the room giving them orders. "Drop to your knees and crawl out of there."

"Do what he says," "Christopher yelled to Daniel. "Let's get out of here."

Just as Daniel was about to crawl for the door, a bright light flashed in the center of the largest crystal bowl.

Daniel stopped crawling, staying perfectly still in a crouched position. A second later another light flashed in the second largest bowl. Almost instantaneously the next bowl lit up and then the next. Soon the whole room was full of light as every crystal from the largest to the smallest was filled with a strange white light.

Slowly, the crystals began to play in beautiful harmony as they each received their light. Steadily, the music became more organized and... more amazing. Soon all of the crystals were playing together in perfect union... and the ship was now in complete control.

When Captain Justo saw what was happening, he motioned wildly for the boys to crawl to him. But just as they started inching forward, the lights started to move. He put his hands up, motioning for them to stay still.

The lights circled inside their crystal centers and the music made a similar harmonic movement. A few more seconds passed; then, all at once in a unified motion, the bowls rose slowly from their nests and gathered like little fireflies in the center of the room, dancing around each other as if they were taking a Sunday walk in the park.

They calmly mingled a few seconds then suddenly crashed into each other, creating one swirling pool of light. At that moment energy beams shot through the room like lightning. Thunder followed each lightning bolt, and an earsplitting musical blast rang in the air and all the lights became one giant, radiant glow of brilliance.

Christopher was terrified. He had just witnessed something he was pretty sure wasn't supposed to happen. Daniel was petrified as well. It was simple to talk about seeing alien technology, but when a lightning blast struck so close it singed the hairs on his head, it wasn't so easy.

The light was motionless for a few seconds, then it started to wander around the room. Phantasm-like, it passed through the bowls, oozing around the machinery without stopping. It wandered around the room without direction until, sensing the two boys, it headed towards them.

"It's c-c-coming toward us," Daniel stammered.

This was the third time in the same day he felt like his life was over. He held perfectly still as the phantasm hovered over them, surrounding their bodies with wisps of light.

"It's all right," Captain Justo said softly, "don't move. This is what we've been trying to get the computer to do for the last two days, only under more controlled conditions, of course. But now everything is going to be all right... just don't move."

Captain Justo looked calm, but Christopher was still horrified. He didn't dare do anything but obey.

The ghostlike creature rolled another wisp of light over them like a trail of smoke from a newly doused campfire. Now, pulling its steamy smoke back into itself, a transformation began. Four tentacles formed out of the centered light and two large eyeballs appeared in a thin transparent skin.

Daniel had wished for real space monsters, but when he actually saw one he wasn't so calm. He put his hands in front of his face and screamed.

"Don't touch it!" Captain Justo yelled.

But, it was too late. Daniel started batting the eerie tentacles with his hands. Each hostile movement made the computer monster more furious. It made a deafening roar and the whole ship started rocking back and forth again like a drunken sailor.

"Get out of there!" Captain Justo commanded at the top of his voice.

He crawled into the room, grabbed Christopher by the collar and, with almost super-human strength, dragged him out the door and shoved him towards the opening in the hall.

"Stay there!" he commanded. Christopher did his best to obey but he was sliding all over the place.

Captain Justo entered the crystal room for another rescue, but couldn't see Daniel anywhere.

"Daniel," he yelled, "where are you?"

"I'm over here," Daniel screamed. "Get me out of here!"

Captain Justo looked up and quickly realized why his ground search was unsuccessful... Daniel was hovering in the middle of the air surrounded by the monster's light.

"I see you. I'll be there in a second!"

Captain Justo crawled under the trapped boy, grabbing his foot. It wouldn't budge.

"Get it off me!" the boy screamed in a panic. "I can barely breathe. Get it off me!"

"I can do it, but it might hurt a little."

Captain Justo took out something that looked like a blaster and aimed it directly at Daniel's chest.

"Don't shoot me," Daniel yelled, "shoot the monster!"

Too late.

Captain Justo pulled the trigger and a blue electric light leapt from its barrel, smashing into Daniel's chest. He groaned in pain as the electricity crackled all over him...

but the light blob screamed its own disapproval and let go of the boy. Daniel fell to the ground in a heap as the light darted to the other end of the room to avoid another painful encounter.

Without wasting any time, Captain Justo grabbed Daniel by the foot, dragging him out of the room. As soon as they were out, the door automatically closed.

"You can stabilize that computer now," Captain Justo said to the same unknown shipmate.

"It will partially stabilize in a few moments," the voice calmly responded over the spaceship's intercom system, "but return to the bridge at once. I am unable to hold her alone for long."

"Are you all right?" Captain Justo asked Daniel as he was coming to his senses.

"Am I all right? When the pain in my chest stops throbbing, I'll let you know. Did you have to shoot me?"

"I just zapped you a little. I can put you back in the crystal room if you'd like. I'm sure the starboard computer holograph won't mind."

"Don't you dare," Daniel said painfully. "I hope I never see it again."

"I doubt we'll be so lucky."

Suddenly the whole ship started rocking, diving up and down. "Hold on to me," Captain Justo commanded both boys; he seemed to be able to walk without sliding around, even with the frantic rocking.

"Command your shoes to stabilize, then follow me up the stairs as soon as you can. If that doesn't work, crawl if you have to. When you get to the foot of the stairs I'll come get you. Just call for me."

With that he turned around, ran down the hall, and disappeared up the stairwell.

Daniel was pale with pain. He crawled over to Christopher, grabbing his leg. "Help me," he said pathetically, "I don't want to die."

Christopher felt a newfound confidence grow inside himself. He looked at his shoes and shouted, "Stabilize!"

In an instant, the shoes seemed to be made of rocks. They stuck to the floor, even though it was moving up and down. He grabbed Daniel by the arm and slowly dragged him down the hall toward where he'd seen Captain Justo disappear.

When they finally got to the foot of the stairs Daniel pointed up and whispered to his brother, "You call for him. I want him to shoot you this time."

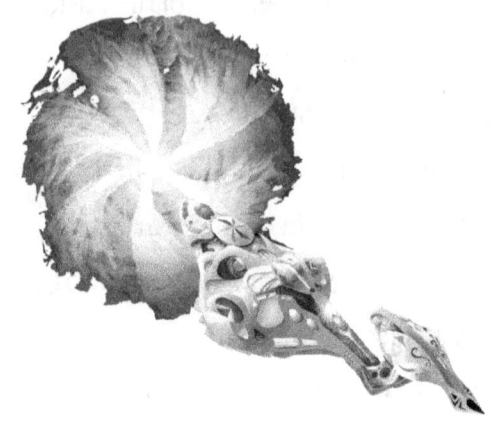

Emergency Escape

The Isian was still rocking back and forth as wildly as before, and neither boy could keep a firm enough grip on the banister to climb even the first three steps. The staircase swept up three tall flights in a circular fashion with three landings that opened to three different floors. At the top of the staircase, in the ceiling, was another shallow chandelier just like in the transporter room.

"Climb up the stairs," Daniel urged. "Go to him; you're the oldest."

"I wish I could. I can't even get up the first step; the floor keeps falling underneath me," Christopher said.

Emergency Escape

Finally pulling all his courage together, the elder brother yelled as loud as he could, "We can't get up the stairs; come and get us."

"There you are," a voice boomed from above them. "Stand back, I'll shoot right down to get you."

"Don't shoot me again," Daniel pleaded, his blood running cold. "I'm sorry I touched the crystal things. I promise I won't touch anything else."

Suddenly a blue light came on in the center of the circular staircase just like the one in the transporter room. Originating three stories up, it beamed all the way down to the bottom floor where the boys were standing. Moments later Captain Justo stepped out of the light and grabbed both boys by their shirts, pulling them into the levitation beam.

"I don't have to shoot you. We're going to blow up long before I'll have the chance to do that," he said, looking up into the light. "Levitate, fourth floor."

The bottom floor sank out of sight as strange lights and symbols flashed past them as the three whizzed straight up. In less than a second they were hovering on the fourth floor. Captain Justo walked out of the levitation beam, then reached over and pulled both boys out of the light. The ship was still rocking back and forth so violently that Daniel couldn't keep his balance long enough to walk anywhere.

"We have the gravitation system working again," Captain Justo told them, sliding back into his captain's chair, "So just say 'stabilize' to your boots and you'll be able to walk."

"Stable ice, what's stable ice?" Daniel asked as he was sliding all over uncontrollably.

"Just say it," Christopher yelled.

"Fine, I'll say it, stable ice." The moment he voiced the command his shoes stuck to the ground, and he was able to stand up.

"No more questions," a gruff, mechanical-sounding voice said.

Captain Justo pointed. "Sit in those chairs and stay out of the way."

Daniel hadn't noticed the other man in the control room at first, but with his shoes creating enough gravity for him to walk, he was able to get a better look.

"That's not a man," Daniel whispered to Christopher. "It's a robot."

"I can see that," Christopher said quietly. "Just stay calm."

Emergency Escape

The boys were right. The other worker was a robot... with a body that glimmered like a gold watch. As they looked closer, they could see his body was crafted in all different colors of gold from white to amber to nearly red; but it was still all pure gold.

"I have temporarily stabilized the engines for now, but it is uncertain how long they will hold," the robot said, making verbal as well as musical commands to the computer. "If the human young refuse to sit down, shall I use more convincing methods to get their cooperation?"

"I'm convinced," Christopher gasped as he ran for a chair. Daniel shrieked and dove for another.

"He's an alien," Daniel said, choking on his words.

"He's a golden alien," Christopher shot back. "Now just shut up and stay alive."

"Boom is a humanoid robot, not an alien," Captain Justo said as he started to energetically play a keyboard. "Of course, in a purely technical sense, I am an alien to your planet myself, so he might be considered an alien robot. But he only bites when boys don't do what he says."

Daniel's eyes got wide as he quickly buried himself into the depths of his seat.

"I beg your pardon. I never bite, I only nibble," the robot corrected.

Suddenly the ship made another violent jerk.

"Here we go again!" Captain Justo yelled. "Activate acceleration protection seats."

"We are too close to the Earth for the kind of repairs we have to make," Boom said, as the ship rocked back and forth. "Furthermore, we may only have a few seconds of control before the starboard engine infects the whole main frame computer."

"I get your point!" Captain Justo yelled, trying to be heard over the noise of the out-of-control engine. "Let's use those seconds and get as far away from the hard ground as possible. Initiate emergency escape."

"Emergency escape initiated," Boom responded. "We are ascending."

Captain Justo grimaced and held onto his chair. "As fast as possible, Boom. Have you boys ever seen a cork popped out of a bottle? Prepare to be the cork."

True to his word, the ship turned on its side and exploded straight up into the air, accelerating so fast that the air in the ship pressed against their bodies with an immense G-force. Fortunately, the acceleration protection devices in the control center chairs wrapped around the human travelers to protect them from much of the massive force of their blast-off.

Emergency Escape

Reaching the speed of sound in just two seconds, the ship sent a sonic boom that rattled every window in town and caused a thunderous roar as it pushed through the sky, creating a vacuum that sucked up air.

"Visual reference," Captain Justo squeaked, barely able to say anything.

At his command a large panel of screens in front of the captain's chair turned into a panoramic view of the ground below, showing the houses and trees fading out of sight. The river flowing through the town became a tiny, pencil-thin line, disappearing into the larger scene of mountain ranges and valleys.

The Isian continued to gain speed; Daniel could barely breathe, the seat was holding him so tightly. He tried to scream, but all he could manage was an agitated wheeze. Captain Justo was as helpless as the two boys. The hard grip of his command chair saved him from suffocating, but it also made him unable to move an inch.

Thirty seconds passed and Boom, who seemed to be unaffected by the speed, was still busily controlling the velocity of the ship. A few more seconds went by and a view of the earth filled the screen.

"Another few seconds," Boom announced as he continued sending furious commands to the only functioning engine. "Six, five, four, three, two, and one... engine off."

The ear-splitting whine of the engines abruptly stopped and the Isian settled into a low orbit among earth's existing satellites. The full view of the earth wasn't visible at first, but with several blinks they could finally see the whole blue planet spinning under them.

Christopher's eyes were watery from the incredible acceleration and, when the chair eventually released its grip, he was able to take his first full breath. He took off his glasses and rubbed them across his shirt to get the fog off before putting them back on. As he regained his breath he blurted, "What is going on? I don't think anyone here has the slightest idea how to operate a spaceship. I want off this pile of junk!"

"Would you like to be put off, now?" Boom asked. "I can arrange to open a cargo door for you."

Christopher's face turned red at his own hot-tempered remark as he sank back in his chair, vowing to keep his mouth shut.

"Shut down all systems except life support," Captain Justo commanded as he got out of his chair and walked toward the two boys, his hands curled into fists at his waist.

"When you touched the crystal bowls, you sent the whole engine out of balance and caused the catastrophe we are presently in. I would appreciate it if you didn't yell at my navigator. He's the only crewmember I have to help get us out of this mess. Do you understand?"

"Yes sir," Christopher said rather softly. "I'm sorry I let Daniel into the engine room. It's really all my fault."

"I'm sorry too," said a repentant Daniel. "I even had to be told to flush the toilet. I hope I haven't ruined everything."

"Everything is not ruined." Boom interjected with assurance. "All of the sanitation facilities still function. Other than that, the rest of the system is going to have to be completely rebooted."

"What about Fanny?" Captain Justo asked Boom. "Shouldn't we let her know what we are about to do?"

"I have already informed her to use the holographic image to report to the command center," Boom said efficiently.

In the center of the room a light rose from an eight-foot circle. In the middle of this pale blue light a middle-aged woman stepped out holding a clipboard.

"Sanitation reporting, sir," She said crisply. "Awaiting orders." "It's the mean woman from the bathroom," Daniel gasped as he sank a little deeper in his chair.

Boom addressed the hologram directly. "We are about to shut down every computer system except yours. The life support system needs to remain operational."

"I understand," she said. "Is there anything else?" "No," Boom answered. "You are dismissed." Seconds later the woman disappeared. "She's the meanest woman I've ever met," Daniel whispered.

"She's not really a woman," Captain Justo explained, "she's a holographic humanoid, just like what we are trying to get the starboard computer to become."

Captain Justo got back in his chair and then turned to give a few instructions to the boys. "This will take about 45 minutes, so everyone hold on tight. There's no gravity during the shut down."

With a few short commands the ship lost complete power. The lights dimmed and were replaced by red glowing emergency chemical lights while the artificial gravity that held everything to the floor was replaced by weightlessness. Daniel strapped himself back into his seat to keep from floating away. With the air circulation cut off, the room was now completely silent except for Boom, who was busily sending musical signals to the mainframe computer and its auxiliaries.

"Why are we here?" Christopher finally asked after a minute of complete silence. "Why do you need us so bad? We haven't helped at all. In fact, all we've done is cause one disaster after another."

Captain Justo pushed off from his seat and floated over to where the two boys were sitting. He carefully placed himself between the two of them and floated at eye level, his feet crossed Indian style.

"I need a sample of your DNA. I have to have at least two chains of human DNA to have the starboard engine reactivated," Captain Justo explained. "That monster downstairs is a holographic humanoid created by my starboard engine. You helped me bring him to life."

Captain Justo continued earnestly, "I still need your help. The starboard engine's transformation isn't even close to being complete yet. We have to help him finish his mutations. When he's completely formed and trained he will be a great asset to this ship, but right now he is very dangerous, as Daniel can tell you."

"That's for sure," Daniel agreed. "It felt like he was sucking my bones out. It was almost as bad as being shot by a ray gun."

Portal Eleven

Captain Justo smiled at Daniel. "I already apologized for that. This is a hostile planet for me. I need people I can trust to help me figure out the situation. While Boom is attempting to reboot the computers, tell me more about your Earth."

Daniel was stunned, but he finally got the idea. "It's pretty big," he offered, "and 70 percent of it is covered in water."

Christopher started to laugh but Captain Justo took in the information very seriously. He looked out the window and pointed at the continent spinning below. "What is that landmass below us called? I believe that is where you live."

"Oh, that is North America," Christopher said confidently. "Our country is called The United States of America. It is there in the middle. We are a republic or a democracy or something like that. The top part over there is a friendly country called Canada. They are a democracy, too, only different. We all speak a language called English. Down there is another country called Mexico. I think they are a democracy but they don't speak English, they speak Spanish."

"Sometimes we're not very nice to them," Daniel blurted. "Kinda like how some big brothers treat little brothers."

Christopher glared back and was about to say something rude when Captain Justo cut him off with another question.

"What about the lower continent? Are they a friend or a foe to you?"

"That's South America," Christopher continued. "They are friendly to us. They all speak Spanish too, I think. Brazil is over there and they play really good soccer, I know that much."

Daniel interrupted, "Uh-uh. Brazil speaks Portageese. My teacher said so."

"So do you have any enemies?" Captain Justo asked seriously.

"Not that many on this side of the world," Daniel piped in, "but the other side is loaded with them."

"What do you mean by that?" the captain continued.

"Do you see that land mass over there?" Christopher said, pointing to Europe. "That's where most of our people came from. We didn't start living in America until about 500 years ago. Getting independent was really hard. We had to fight to get it. Even after we won we still had to fight to stay independent."

"So you have a free country?"

"Of course we do," Daniel said proudly. "We live in the United States of America. Our Pledge of Allegiance goes like this." Daniel put his hand on his heart and began solemnly, "I pledge allegiance to the flag of the United States of America, and to the republic for which it stands, one nation under God, invisible, with liberty and justice for all," he misquoted.

A broad smile came over the young captain's face. He looked over at Boom, hoping the robot's sensors had recorded this.

"Well, now I know what kind of people I'm dealing with," he said with a grin. "Any people with a motto like that is a friend of mine. Now I know I can trust you... so let me tell you a little bit about my people."

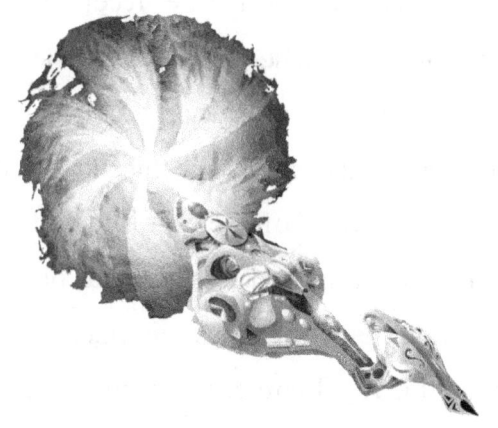

Holographic Humanoid

"I'm not from this planet, as you already know, but I'm also not from this universe," Captain Justo said with a smile. "I'm from a place so far away I don't even have a map big enough to show it to you. Anyway, just about 2,600 years ago, our people were divided into many warring groups and factions. We were uncivilized and unorganized; we were unschooled and backward; we had almost no technologies. We probably would have stayed that way forever if not for a group of colonizers who came from a faraway universe and taught us the right way to live.

"They taught us about basic human needs-that all have a yearning for eternal life, hope, prosperity, growth, security, strength, love, and independence. We learned that these basic needs could only be received by acts of humility, self-improvement, service, knowledge, mercy, purity, peace-making, and sacrifice.

"They taught us many other things, all part of a plan of happiness that centered on life as it is to be found both in the realm of mortal time and eternity. Our people were so grateful we made them our kings and rulers. I am a direct descendent of this royal house, as are many of my people. The royal blood line is dispersed among all of our people and we are proud to be called Isians."

Neither boy moved a muscle. They listened intently and Captain Justo continued his explanation.

"About 2,000 years ago another amazing thing occurred. We were visited by the great Is, King of the Royal Family. He added to our ancestors' wise teachings and organized the kingdom to bless all humanity. He gave us the responsibility to expand into every galaxy and teach all people the ways of Is.

"But to our great sadness, this great teacher did not stay with us. He said he had many other lands and other people to visit as well. We wept as he was about to leave, but he promised he would return. We are still waiting."

"So if you were so backward and uneducated how did you ever get this advanced?" Christopher asked.

"It didn't happen overnight," Captain Justo continued. "It took a long time for the Royal Family to help us get over all of our bad habits. Over time we had fewer wars and the people became prosperous. And because there was more peace we had time to devote to the arts, science, and discovery. Each century we slowly became more technologically advanced. We went from driving around in horse-drawn carts to piloting rocket-propelled vehicles to our nearest moon and beyond."

"How long did it take you to learn to travel at the speed of light?" Daniel asked.

"About 500 terra-years," Captain Justo answered, and then paused. "Well we haven't actually ever reached the speed of light," he admitted. "But we have found other, faster ways of getting around."

"What's a terra-year?" asked Christopher.

"A terra-year is a year for a standard terra-planet," he answered. "And before you ask, a terra-planet is one like yours. All measurements are defined by the time it takes a planet of this type to orbit around the star it belongs to. Planets with life on them are terra-planets. Does that help?"

"Cool," Daniel cooed. "As soon as you get your ship fixed, will you take us to one?"

"That could be a problem," Captain Justo said slowly. "We are having a few technical difficulties."

"Well, after you fix your computers and get your maps up, then could you show us?"

"If you were prepared, I could show you a few in your own universe, but not in mine," the captain said hesitantly.

"Why not?" Daniel questioned.

"Because," Boom interrupted, "we are unable to determine where our universe fits in relation to your universe."

"You're lost," Christopher laughed. "How could you get lost?"

"Anything is possible." Captain Justo frowned. "Anyway, space is a very big place. If I had my father and his crew on board it would be a lot easier."

"Where *are* your father and his crew?" Christopher asked. "I haven't seen another person on board this ship. What did you do, borrow your dad's keys and get lost on the freeway?"

"Well, not quite. It was more like being pushed off a bridge, landing on a strange road, and then looking for help. Unfortunately, I don't know where they are. We've been wandering around your universe for months, trying to figure out where we are and how to get back home. If only my father were here."

"Ah, yes, your father," Boom interrupted again. "What a fine man. Lorenzo Justo is one of the finest captains I ever sailed with."

"Let's not get into that again, Boom. I've told you a hundred times, Lorenzo is my great-grandfather and not my father. I am Marion James Justo, not Marion Thomas Justo."

"Yes, yes," Boom responded patiently. "I am glad to see your humor is unimpaired at a time like this. These computers will be back up and running in no time at all."

"What is that all about?" Christopher asked curiously.

"He thinks I'm my grandfather," Captain Justo whispered while floating closer to the two boys. "Nothing I can do or say has been able to convince him otherwise. He even thinks I tampered with the medical computers to change my DNA files just to make it all the more believable."

"Why won't he believe you?" Daniel whispered. "Is he broken or something?"

"I don't think so," Captain Justo whispered. "But even if he is broken, he is such an important part of the ship that if I tried to shut him down, the whole ship would probably fly completely out of control."

"Doesn't that make working together kind of weird?" Daniel asked.

"It's lonely mostly," Captain Justo lamented. "For six months no one has said my name believing I am who I say I am. It would be really nice to hear my name again."

"So how did you lose control of your ship?" Christopher asked. "I don't think crashing into things is a normal activity for a spaceship, is it?"

"Not at all. After we found ourselves trapped in this strange, uncharted universe, we started to map it, in hopes of finding familiar territory. Our mapping was going slowly and the universe seemed to be devoid of any human life; and then, a few days ago, we heard faint radio signals coming from your planet. We were so happy, we set our course for your planet's position and arrived near your moon. Unfortunately, we weren't in your gravity field for 10 seconds before we were attacked by your planet's harmonic defense system."

"Harmonic defense system? What the heck is that?"

"I don't even know what the word means," Daniel confessed.

"That doesn't surprise me too much. Neither of you are very old, but don't you know anything about harmonics?" Captain Justo looked puzzled. "Every advanced civilization knows that harmonics is the science that deals with the relationships between musical frequencies. Even gravity follows these Harmonic Rules. How can you not know this already?"

Christopher started to laugh. "You are telling me that gravity is musical? That doesn't even make sense. I've never seen music have an effect on anything, let alone gravity."

"Have you ever heard about a soprano breaking a glass with her voice?" Captain Justo questioned.

"I've heard of that," Christopher admitted. "But I thought it was all just a joke."

"It's not a joke," Justo insisted. "Breaking glass isn't very important, but music... it is very powerful. The whole universe is controlled by music. It's so important to space travel that the Isian is run by musical programs. The life-support system, the computers, and even the harmonic drives are all controlled by music."

"I'd like to see the harmonic drives," Daniel said excitedly.

"Believe me, you already have," the captain grimaced. "The room with the crystal bowls is the harmonic drive room. Each bowl is like a piston in an engine, musically tuned to the gravitational field of whatever mass it is pushing against. When the harmonic frequency of the spaceship matches the harmonic frequency of the planet or mass below, then gravity pushes instead of pulls. At the right frequency the Isian becomes as buoyant as a balloon at the bottom of a swimming pool."

"So what happened when Daniel and I touched the crystal bowls?" Christopher asked, a little afraid to know the answer.

"When you touched the bowl you changed the harmonic frequency of the ship," Captain Justo explained. "We immediately lost control and started to fall from the sky. In the attempt to re-establish the correct frequency, the entire starboard computer program crashed."

"I'm sorry," Daniel moaned. "I didn't mean to wreck your whole computer system."

"It's not all his fault," Christopher finally admitted. "I went into the harmonic drive room first; he just followed me."

"Well, what's done is done. I should have been paying closer attention to you. Besides, the starboard engine was damaged before you came on board."

"You really did us a great favor," the golden robot said to show he had been listening while waiting for another program to load. "When the program crashed I did an emergency reboot and it accidentally jump-started the holographic humanoid program. We had been working for two days to get that program to work, but we were missing another human DNA strand.

"The computer already had Captain Justo's DNA on file, and it got the other strand directly from Daniel when it had him hanging from the ceiling. I know Captain Justo wasn't looking forward to the initial contact with the hologram, so it was fortunate that Daniel made first contact for him."

"Do you mean that monster was supposed to grab and almost kill me?" Daniel blurted.

"It was supposed to be created, but not like that," the captain insisted. "I was prepared to be the major DNA donor. It would have been better that way. Now I have a holographic humanoid program that matches your dominant DNA and not mine. I just hope we can control it. I guess we'll find out when we reboot the computer."

"What happens then?" Daniel asked.

"When the computer is rebooted," Boom explained, "we will splice another piece of Captain Justo's DNA into the program. When that is completed we will take a piece of your DNA and do the same thing. If all goes well the program will develop into a strong, virus-resistant holographic humanoid. It should be capable of taking musical commands and running the starboard engine's harmonic drive."

Christopher was still a little confused. "All of this because of a musical attack. I don't get it."

"I thought you would know more about harmonics," Captain Justo said, puzzled. "After all, it was your planet's harmonic defense system that caused the Isian to crash in the first place."

"I still don't know what you're talking about," Christopher replied. "Our country doesn't even have a tested strategic missile defense system, so I know we couldn't have a harmonic defense system."

"Well, what do you call this, then?" Captain Justo challenged.

He floated over to his chair and came back with a bag full of small marble-sized crystals.

"I recorded one of the nastier musical viruses on this crystal. You tell me what it is."

He put the marble in a slide-card-like player and put it into Christopher's hand. Instantly the music filled his head and he started to laugh.

"This isn't a secret harmonic defense program," he chuckled. "This is Heavy Metal. I can't stand music this hard. I had a music recorder full of it my uncle gave me that I never listened to, until Brilliance here lost it, but some of my friends love it. I think I even had this song."

"Let me hear it," Daniel begged. When the disk player found its way into Daniel's hand, he immediately started to bounce his head wildly. "I love this song," Daniel screamed over the sound of the music. "This is from my favorite band, Seven of Spades. All my friends love this song."

The Captain pushed off from Daniel's seat where he was still bouncing to the music, and floated over to where Boom was making his last commands to the injured computers.

"What do you think?" he whispered to Boom.

Boom looked over at the two boys fighting over the music player.

"Captain," he began, "if these two uneducated boys know the name of this computer virus, then I sincerely doubt it is part of an organized defense system."

"So what you are saying?" the Captain asked. "Are you suggesting the most sophisticated starship in the civilized universe has been defeated by children's music?"

"Not defeated," Boom responded, "only bruised. We are still alive, and when this computer reboots we will be alive and well for many years to come.

"I am ready to re-engage the computers now," Boom continued, "please turn that computer virus off so it doesn't accidentally infect the whole system again."

Captain Justo agreed and floated over to where Daniel was holding onto the player with both hands while Christopher was trying to take it from him.

"I'll take that," Captain Justo said as he pried the musical player from both of their hands. "We are about to engage the computers. Sit securely in your seats. If you are not sitting down properly, you may fly off and hit your head on the ceiling."

Without hesitation, both boys settled deeply into their seats and watched as Boom initiated the final commands to call the computers back on line. A moment of silence passed before a familiar ring resounded throughout the ship.

Captain Justo and Boom were obviously relieved. The lights came on at full power and the gravity returned. Now Boom commanded the port engine to engage and it did so without incident.

Then, as he started to engage the starboard harmonic drive, the engine went crazy and the Isian began rocking back and forth wildly, as it had before. Boom immediately ordered the harmonic drive to shut down, but nothing happened. He tried again, but again there was no response. Suddenly a massive musical blast was heard down in the belly of the ship.

Captain Justo jumped out of his seat and ran to the transporter beam next to the stairs. He was about to go down the levitator, but stopped, then started walking slowly backward instead.

A red, wet image walked into the room with two bugging eyes rolling around in a jellyfish-like head. It looked straight at Captain Justo and then circled its two tentacle-like arms around his chest without touching him, pulsating with his heartbeat.

"Do you remember the holographic humanoid we have been talking about?" Captain Justo whispered to

Boom quietly. "Well, I'd like you to meet him. Do you have any idea what we should do now?"

"Hold still," Boom commanded. "The only thing it can see is vibration. If you touch it we may not ever be able to control it."

"Believe me," Justo confided. "I don't want to touch it."

"It feels the harmonic motion of your body," Boom said quietly. "It may recognize your DNA patterns. Just let it finish what it is doing. It is learning how a human body functions."

Captain Justo slowly nodded his head. The monster slowly nodded its own in the same way and the near-formless image started mutating. The tentacles slowly took on a human form as they moved around the Captain's body, still without touching him. The jellyfish head gurgled and popped as it developed a skull from the inside out.

Daniel was speechless; he didn't dare move a muscle. He had wanted to see a real alien, but now he was watching one and he *really* didn't want it to coming any closer. It had some of his DNA? What if it came to him next? He watched terrified as the tentacles underneath the monster started developing bones to match those of Captain Justo's.

"You're doing a good job," Boom said quietly to the Captain. "In a few minutes he will take on your form completely. After that maybe we can communicate with him."

"I hope that happens soon, I don't know how much longer I can stand still."

"I hope that happens soon," the monster copied, "I don't know how much longer I can stand still."

Now muscle started to form over the skeleton, then skin over the top of that. It was almost formed when Daniel, unable to hold back, sneezed.

The sound broke the silence in the room and the nearly formed image left Captain Justo and walked over to the boys' chairs. It stood over them and looked directly into their eyes one at a time, then stopped in front of Daniel, who was as stiff as a petrified tree. Daniel's eyes were open as wide as they could go... the monster made the same expression, as the skin around his eyelids, nose, and ears began to fill in.

The hologram walked over to Boom, but expressed no interest whatever. Then it returned to Captain Justo... a perfectly formed young man.

The boys were a little embarrassed by the fact that the figure was completely naked; at the same time the creature somehow sensed it was different and started creating clothes for itself.

It walked around Captain Justo again in a curious manner, stopping right in front of him and motioning towards his pocket. With a curl of his new finger, the music player slowly rose from the Captain's pocket.

"Don't let him play that recording," Boom commanded. "He may look uncontrollable now, but at least he is virus-free. We're doomed if he gets infected with that virus again."

Captain Justo grabbed the player, taking the infected crystal off it. He quickly dropped the stone into his pocket and handed the player to the hologram.

Outraged, the hologram roared sounds. "I hope that happens soon," the hologram screamed, repeating Captain Justo's words without understanding their meaning. "I don't know how much longer I can stand still."

"Put another crystal on the player," Boom instructed. "Let him hear something soothing."

Captain Justo slowly walked over to his seat and pulled out a handful of crystals from a drawer. He took one, put it on the player, and quiet soothing music filled the room. The hologram pulled a face, causing the crystal to fly off the player. He motioned for another crystal which was placed on the player. This time a lively waltz was heard... again the hologram made a terrible look and tossed it on the ground.

"Let him listen to everything," Boom instructed. "He's a harmonic program. If we can find out what he likes, I can program him through the music."

Captain Justo played every kind of music he had. He played classical music, polkas, minuets, quadrilles, sonnets, chansons, chants, and hymns, but nothing worked. One musical selection after another found its way to the floor. In barely minutes, Captain Justo had offered every musical selection he had available on the bridge, but the hologram didn't respond to any of them.

"What now?" the Captain begged. "I've let him listen to everything I have. What other kinds of music *are* there?"

"I am out of solutions," Boom replied. "There aren't any other forms of music that I am aware of."

"What do you mean by that?" Christopher objected. "You haven't played any kind of rock and roll. You haven't played him any funk or swing or jazz. I know tons of stuff that you haven't even tried yet."

"Your tribal music got us into this mess," Boom said coldly, "and actually, I do not call it music at all, it is more of a menace."

"Our music isn't a menace!" Daniel yelled. "It's awesome. Maybe some of it's bad, but most of it's really cool."

"I hope you're right," Captain Justo conceded, "but I don't know anything about your music. Maybe after we've studied it more we could find something the hologram would respond to in a positive way."

Boom made a low, mechanical sound. He obviously didn't agree.

Now the hologram raised both hands and motioned, trying to make the crystal rise out of Captain Justo's pocket, but the Captain held his ground.

"You can't have that," the captain insisted.

The hologram was getting restless and tried to get the crystal again, but Captain Justo held it even tighter. Suddenly, with the tug of war, the entire ship rocked back and forth.

"No matter what happens, don't let him have that stone," Boom commanded, furiously trying to counteract the holographic engine's commands with the one port engine that was still operating.

Holographic Humanoid

"Can you stop this thing?" Captain Justo pleaded. "He's lifting me right off the ground to get at it. I don't know how much longer I can keep it from him."

"I'll try to talk to him in a language he can understand," Boom said confidently.

The robot stood away from his computer, talking in a wild array of musical tones; but the hologram countered with another set of musical tones, pushing Boom across the room by simply raising his hand.

"I thought you said this was a hologram," Christopher sputtered. "A hologram can't move things."

"This one can," Boom answered while picking himself up off the floor. "He is a holographic humanoid, but he has complete control of the ship's starboard engine. Anything the harmonic drive can do, he can do. He has the harmonic energy of the whole ship at his command. As long as he is running freely on this ship, nothing is out of his control except for the sanitation program. It's the only program not connected to the mainframe computer."

"Flush him down the toilet," Daniel yelled, "that'll show him!"

"Flush him down the toilet?" Christopher jeered. "That's the stupidest thing I've ever heard."

"That's it!" Captain Justo yelled struggling to face Boom. "A holographic imager displays holographic images from the different computer systems, right?"

"Yes," Boom responded, not understanding where the Captain was going with his question.

"If so, then why can't a holographic imager download a holographic humanoid from one program and capture it in another? We can't beam him to the main-frame computer because the starboard engine is directly connected to the main frame and he'll escape, but we could beam him into the sanitation computer. It's independent of the main frame computer, isn't it?"

"I understand, Captain," Boom said confidently. "We capture and hold the holographic humanoid with Fanny in the sanitation computer until we discover how to tame it."

Christopher and Daniel had seen the holographic imager used once before when the Sanitation Engineer, Fanny, was informed of the computer shut down. It was a tool used to display three-dimensional images to the officers of the command center and was useful for communication as well as for mapping. Located in the center of the room, it took up an area about eight feet in diameter. The inside circle was ornately carved with the same interlocking snowflake displayed on Captain Justo's uniform. It was beautiful, like everything else inside the ship.

Captain Justo slowly backed toward the circle engraved in the center of the command post floor. The monster, concentrating on getting the crystal, tried to keep him from moving, but Captain Justo slowly inched towards the center of the circle.

"A little farther," Boom urged.

Captain Justo struggled to move into the circle. His resistance was upsetting the half-finished hologram so it moved closer, as if to be more intimidating. It was just what Captain Justo wanted it to do... step by step, they wrestled with each other until the creature was completely within the circle, still tugging on the music crystal and making terrible groaning noises.

"Perfect, stay right there."

With a short musical command the holographic imager came to life, causing the entire circle to fill up with light and the holographic humanoid dropped Captain Justo, roaring his disapproval. It tried desperately to get out of the light but no matter how loud it yelled or how hard it tried, it couldn't escape.

Boom made a few more musical commands and a third figure appeared in the center of the circle. It was Daniel's least favorite Sanitation Engineer.

"Hello, Fanny," Boom said respectfully. "Please take this holographic humanoid computer program and keep it contained for a few days."

"Oh, I would rather not," she responded firmly. "I have an incredible rust problem with the third floor pipes. This ship hasn't been serviced for years."

"I can appreciate your technical problems," Captain Justo said firmly (he knew how to communicate with his sanitation program), but unfortunately if you don't do this you will not only be disobeying a direct order but you will also be responsible for the massive destruction he is about to perform. This holographic humanoid is planning to blow up every pipe on the ship."

"Destroy my pipes?" she questioned sternly, "in that case I would be delighted. Come here you nasty program, I have some manners to teach you."

She grabbed the holographic humanoid by its holographic ear and disappeared into the floor.

"I wouldn't want to mess with Fanny," Captain Justo said with a smile, "she even scares me sometimes."

"Tell me about it," Daniel agreed, still hiding in his chair.

Moments later the entire room filled with the smell of sewer gas as all the toilets overflowed and the water in the walls swished around violently. Captain Justo looked over at Boom, trying not to throw up. "Take care of that," he groaned.

"All systems appear to be fully functional," Boom said after a quick systems check. "It appears Fanny is having trouble keeping our new young friend contained, but she assures me all will be well. The port engine is operating perfectly; we have half harmonic power with the starboard engine offline, but we are still connected to the emergency ionic engines, so I think we have plenty of power to get these two boys back home. Prepare for a standard orbit and reentry."

"You have done everything I asked you to do," Captain Justo said to the two boys who were looking green from the putrid smell surrounding them. "I've put you in way too much danger already. Sit up straight in your chairs and strap in. Let's take you home. Boom, *please* do something about this smell... I'm getting sick."

"There's nothing we can do, sir. Fanny reports that the holographic humanoid is very dangerous and she has temporarily confined it to the sewer system. But she does assure me nothing you smell is toxic."

At that, Boom activated the harmonic drive and a familiar ringing entered the boys' ears. Captain Justo would have breathed a sigh of relief, but the putrid smell coming from the ventilation system *was* truly making him ill. The sound of banging pipes rattled the ship, and puffs of re-filtered green gas continued to leak from the ventilation system.

"There are emergency bags on the sides of your chairs," he told the two boys as his gag reflex overcame him and he vomited into a bag. "Initiate re-entry on my mark," he groaned, "Three, two, one," he threw up again and wiped the dribble from his chin... "mark."

Get a sneak peek of the next exciting adventure!

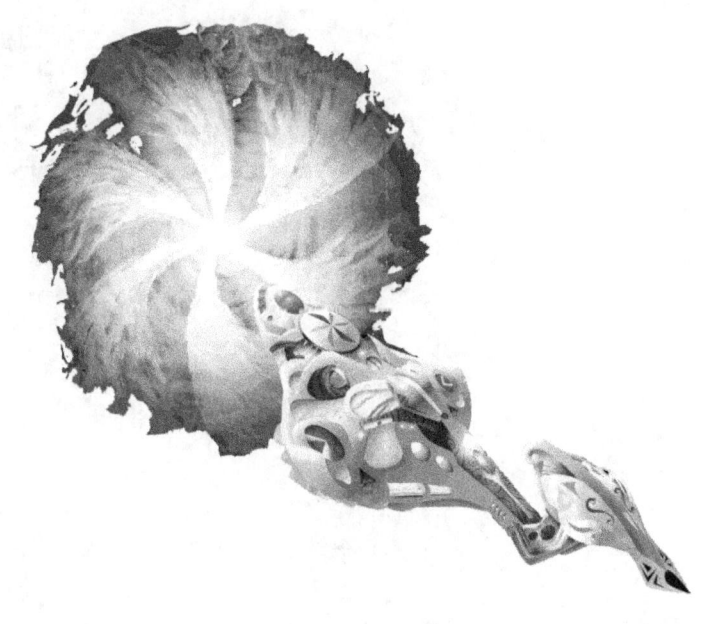

Sneak Peek Captain Justo Log 1.2

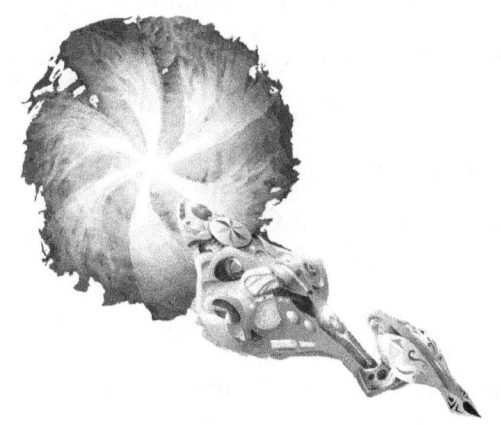

Heavy Metal Attack

The journey back took a lot longer than the two boys expected. Christopher sat in his chair trying to understand the musical code Boom was entering into the computer, while Daniel tried to stay awake... he wasn't very successful.

"We better not get too close to a city," Captain Justo told Boom. "I don't want to be seen this time."

"Or heard," Boom added.

"Especially heard," the Captain agreed. "I'll bet the sonic boom from a few hours ago woke up a few babies. I hope we didn't break too many windows."

"Not as many windows as we would have broken if the Isian had exploded," Boom assured him.

"Don't remind me."

"I don't get why," Christopher butted in. "I doubt those crystal bowls would have made much of an explosion."

"The destruction of the harmonic accelerators wouldn't have caused any damage by themselves," the Captain agreed, "but if our ionic power rods had exploded it would have most likely destroyed your whole town."

Christopher was about to ask more questions when the command screen started flashing warning lights. Boom quickly brought up a new program window—a cutout of the Isian with a wide energy shield surrounding it. Torpedo-like objects were bombarding it at regular intervals, eating away at the shield.

"It's just like before," Boom warned. "I have our harmonic shields up to maximum power, but those harmonic viruses are still trying to eat through it."

"This can't be happening," Captain Justo moaned. "I've never heard of a harmonic virus getting through a maximum power shield. What's going on here?"

"For some reason our computer system is off balance," Boom said quickly, "but it's not related to the viruses themselves. You had better see this for yourself."

Captain Justo turned his chair back to the command screen and hurriedly pulled up his own version of the same program. "How long before we have harmonic shield failure?" Captain Justo barked.

"Less than three minutes," Boom responded seriously. Now Daniel was wide awake for good. He looked from Boom to Captain Justo. Christopher, however, was busy thinking.

"I have an idea," Captain Justo said confidently. "Let's use the musical blueprint from the virus we recorded on this disk and purposely give ourselves the virus. If we can give it to ourselves in a controlled way and in a small enough dose, maybe the computer can create its own virtual vaccine."

"It might work," Boom agreed as he entered a string of commands into the mainframe computer. "You're out of your mind," Christopher said, coughing from the smell. "I've seen what a virus can do to a computer. Don't do it."

Sneak Peek

"Let me have the virus," Boom commanded, and Captain Justo carefully handed him the stone. The robot put it on the player and, through a wireless device, shot it into the main-frame computer.

Daniel didn't even dare to look this time. He had been close to death so many times in one day that this was just one time too many. A few seconds passed and the lights in the command center started to flicker, then the whole ship seemed to moan like it was sick and getting ready to throw up. A stale stink came from the cooling vents; even the sanitation program was sickened by the virus.

"How much time do we have left?" Captain Justo asked, looking at the incoming viruses on the screen.

"We have 30 seconds until full shield penetration," Boom replied, looking at Captain Justo uneasily.

Captain Justo fed the final portion of the virus into the main-frame computer and then turned the shields to minimum power. The oncoming viruses increased their speed and were ready to slam into the ship just as the lights in the command room turned bright red. At that moment Boom diverted all the power to the front harmonic shield as both Boom and the Captain frantically played piano-instrument boards like they were in a concert recital.

Sneak Peek

Christopher and Daniel looked on helplessly. Each second was so important that at times they felt like the ship would explode out from under them in a fiery ball of flames.

Finally, after 10 seconds of frantic playing, the last of the viruses had been pushed back and were no longer a threat. Captain Justo leaned back in his chair completely exhausted. Looking back at the two boys, he released a deep sigh.

"All the incoming viruses were different variations of the same virus," Captain Justo finally explained. "By giving the ship a small piece of the virus at controlled intervals, it was able to discover the poisonous parts and inoculate itself. I don't think we will be having any more difficulty with your planet's harmonic defense system-real or not."

* * * * * * * * * *

After a short while, the ship moved into the shadow of a large cloud. The panoramic view of the earth below replaced the emergency screen and, near the center of the screen, Christopher recognized a mountain range with the river running through it.

"There's our town!" Daniel said excitedly. "I didn't think I'd ever see it again. You space guys really know how to make an exciting ride."

"We do our best," Captain Justo smiled, "but we space guys don't like making it *too* exciting."

Captain Justo released the emergency status and disabled the chairs' massive acceleration protection program. Stepping out of his seat, he stretched a few moments, then walked over to Boom and put his hand on his metal shoulder.

"Let's hover at about 10,000 feet," he said quietly. "Before we return them to Earth let's check our surveillance probe and see if everything is safe."

He turned to the boys and finished his thoughts. "We've been gone for about three hours. I'm going to activate a surveillance probe I left in the field where we first met this afternoon. It recorded any activity at the crash site during the time we've been gone. If anything out of the ordinary has happened we'll know it. Also, I'd appreciate it if you'd tell me if you recognize anyone."

The holographic image whined up to full power and, in the center of a snowflake-looking circle in the command center, displayed a perfect three-dimensional representation of the field next to the river.

Sneak Peek

"Contact made with the surveillance probe," Boom announced mechanically, as if nothing interesting had even happened that day. "Downloading all information recorded over the last three hours. Broadcasting holographic images now," he reported.

The holographic imager buzzed again and showed the same field and river as three hours earlier. Fortunately, nothing looked out of the ordinary.

"Fast forward the image," Captain Justo commanded. Boom made a few musical tones and the image went into fast forward. Nothing changed in the first few seconds except for a few birds flying around in a zipping motion. Another uneventful minute passed and then a group of boys walked onto the screen. Their jerky movements bounced around for a second and then stopped.

"I'll rewind and replay it," the Captain said intently. In the imager the boys walked backwards for a second, then froze. The holographic image zoomed in on the boys.

Daniel gasped and fell back into his chair.

"Do you know these boys?" Boom questioned.

"Yeah." He frowned. "That's Benny Strong, and those are his brothers."

About the Author

Stephen Miller was born in Provo, Utah in 1962. While attending high school, Stephen won several statewide debate competitions and received high marks at statewide drama competitions for two years running. His school won the state competition both years.

He met his future wife, crowned Miss Payson, while attending school in Payson, Utah. After graduating with honors, Stephen took on more adventure by joining the

About the Author

Utah Air National Guard. He attended Brigham Young University where he studied Portuguese, Aerospace Studies and Physics. The love of flying machines, languages, and physics are core concepts in his writing. He was a member of the Air Force ROTC for four years.

It was in Sacramento, California while serving in the U.S. Air Force that *Captain Justo from the Planet Is* was first told as a bedtime story to his children. It was so loved that Stephen was urged to write it down, and *Captain Justo from the Planet Is* became a rough draft. Over the years, the manuscript went through further modifications to add depth and meaning to the story.

Stephen took a break from writing Captain Justo and finished his first published book entitled *The Home Buyer's Coaching Clinic*, also published by TriQuest Publishing. The publishing experience was very positive, which encouraged him to keep writing his science fiction work. *Captain Justo from the Planet Is* was completed in the early winter months of 2008. After over 15 years in development, not only the philosophy, but the characters and the final plot of the book were finished.

Stephen has written other works. He wrote the music for "Christmas Time Again" and "Possum City

About the Author

USA" in 1997 and 1998. In 1998, he wrote and produced, "The Peddler's Muse."

Currently he is working on a CD with his wife Edna, a classically-trained vocalist. He also recently completed an MBA from the University of Phoenix which will form much the basis of his next installment of the Isian Series.

Stephen and Edna are the proud parents of seven children and have four grandchildren.

Readers Praise

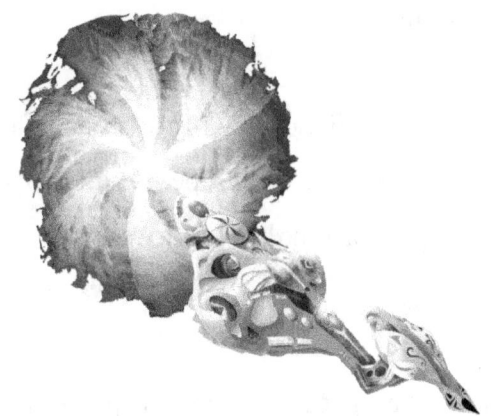

Captain Justo From the Planet Is

It was a wonderful book. I love it. I got my science teacher to look into it. Read it, you'll love it.

Carolee, age 14

This book is one in a trillion. I've read this book three times.

Kobe Black, Age 11

My son read your book, and he said that it was the very best book he has ever read. He's thirteen and he's read all the Harry Potter books, *Eragon*, etc.

Dawn Johnson, Pleasant Grove, Utah; son age 13

Reader's Praise

My grandson loves Captain Justo and can't wait for the next book to come out!

Laura Hall

I love science fiction, and this is one of my favorite ones. I love how they can shrink people and how their ship can travel through worm holes. It is awesome!

Miah

Justo has a spaceship. He can go through portals. He has an Admiral named Aaron. He has a golden spaceship.

Jacob, grade 4

My son who was six at the time LOVED it. He would just sit and listen to me read it to him.

Dana

We are almost done with the book, and my boys have been fascinated with it and VERY disappointed on the nights when I am not able to read it to them. They range in age from seven to fourteen, and each of them is actively engaged in the story. Every night after teeth brushing and family prayer, the cry is "Captain Justo, Captain Justo!"

Reader's Praise

The mystery, intrigue, action, drama, and comedy mix together in an incredible story of spaceships, a dashing young captain, robots, and good vs. evil. You don't just know the good guys are good, you understand the good principles that guide them and that these principles are beneficial to their lives. The great thing is that it is done skillfully and subtly as a part of the story, teaching without preaching, and my children love it!

Richard Brinkworth

It was a great adventure book that I can read over and over.

Patricia Lou

This book is delightful – filled with adventure and excitement as a traveler from space meets up with a family from earth. You will enjoy the interaction of the young boys as they meet and try to help this man from outer space.

Maxine Miller, American Fork, Utah.

The Eight Pearls of Is

- I need Eternal Life: therefore, I must humbly submit to the will of God in all things.

- I need hope: therefore, I must recognize and endure the pain of my mistakes; I must restore any harm, and be determined to improve.

- I need prosperity: therefore, I must meekly serve others.

- I need competence: therefore, I must discover and follow the true path to perfection.

- I need security: therefore, I must obey the laws of economy, society, and family.

- I need strength: therefore, I must purify my body, thoughts, and passions.

- I need love from others: therefore, I must be a peacemaker and extend charity to all.

- I need autonomy: therefore, I must sacrifice for what I believe in and allow others to do the same.